RETURN

'5
OCT 2015
'7

THE VIRGIN'S
PRICE

THE VIRGIN'S PRICE

BY
MELANIE MILBURNE

First published in Great Britain 2006
Large Print edition 2007
Harlequin Mills & Boon Limited,
Eton House, 18-24 Paradise Road,
Richmond, Surrey TW9 1SR

© Melanie Milburne 2006

ISBN-13: 978 0 263 19442 5   BBC 4/4/07
ISBN-10:   0 263 19442 6

Set in Times Roman 16½ on 19 pt.
16-0407-55200

Printed and bound in Great Britain
by Antony Rowe Ltd, Chippenham, Wiltshire

To my sisters, Coralie Margaret McNamara and Jessie Isobel Bohannon. Thank you for your love and support over the years. I love you both very dearly.

CHAPTER ONE

'I CAN'T believe he wrote that about me!' Mia threw the morning's newspaper down in disgust, her grey eyes flashing with rage. 'It's the first real acting job I've had and he completely rubbishes it. My career will be over before it even starts.'

'I wouldn't take it too personally,' Shelley said as she reloaded the café dishwasher. 'Bryn Dwyer rubbishes just about everything. Did you hear him on drive-time radio yesterday? He made a complete fool of the person he was interviewing. It's how he gets the ratings he does. You either love him or you hate him.'

'Well, I *hate* him,' Mia said with feeling. 'I just wish I could have the chance to tell him to his arrogant, stuck-up face.'

'Yeah, well, you never know your luck,' Shelley said as she placed the washing powder in the compartment of the dishwasher. 'He was in here three mornings in a row last week, each time with a different woman. You should have seen the way Tony gushed all over him as if he was royalty. I nearly puked.'

'*In here?*' Mia's eyes began to sparkle with hope. 'Bryn Dwyer?'

Shelley straightened from the dishwasher. 'Listen, Mia, just remember you've only just started and Tony only gave you the job in the first place because I put in such a good word for you. If you so much as—'

'One cappuccino and a double decaf latte on table seven.' Tony Pretelli, the café owner, slapped the order on the counter and scooped up a plate of raisin toast on his way past. 'And make it snappy. Our favourite celebrity is here again this morning.'

'Uh-oh,' Shelley said as she took a quick peek over the counter.

'Who is it?' Mia asked as she peered over Shelley's shoulder. She whistled through her teeth when she caught a glimpse of a tall man with dark brown shiny hair and broad shoulders sitting chatting to an attractive brunette. 'Well, I'll be damned.'

Shelley grabbed her by the arm. 'Don't even think about it, Mia. You know what Tony's like. He'll fire you on the spot if you do anything to upset a customer, celebrity or not.'

Mia unpeeled the waitress's fingers and, giving her a sugar-sweet smile, reached for the coffees the barista on duty had just made. 'I think I'll risk it just this once. Anyway, it will be worth it to get back at that pompous jerk for giving me such a bad review.'

Shelley winced as Mia swept past with the coffees. 'I don't think I can watch this…'

Mia sauntered up to the table where Bryn Dwyer was seated with his back to her. It was a very broad back, she couldn't help noticing, and even though he was wearing a pale blue business shirt she could see the bunching of well-developed muscles through the expensive fabric. His shirt cuffs were rolled up at the wrists, revealing tanned forearms sprinkled with dark masculine hair, and an expensive silver watch on his left wrist. His hair was neither long nor short or straight or curly but somewhere in between, and was styled in a casual manner that suggested his long, tanned fingers had been used as its latest combing tool.

She didn't need to see his face; it had been splashed on the cover of just about every women's magazine for the past month as for the second year in a row he had been awarded the Bachelor of the Year title. His prime-time radio slot and popular weekly column in a Sydney broadsheet gave him the sort of fame and fortune most people only ever dreamed of, but even without that, he was a multimillionaire from some clever property investments he'd made all before he'd hit thirty-two or -three years or so ago.

Mia gave her reflection a quick glance in the mirrors above the booth section of the café on her way past, reassuring herself that he couldn't possibly recognise her from last night's performance. With her shoulder-length blonde hair scraped back in a high pony-tail and no make-up on she looked just like an ordinary café waitress. She gave a mischievous little smile as she mentally rehearsed an Irish accent; even better—a visiting-from-abroad café waitress.

'Top of the mornin' to you both. Now, what do we have here—a cappuccino and a double skinny decaf?' she lilted cheerily, as she hovered by Bryn's elbow.

'Mine is the decaf,' the brunette woman said with a friendly smile.

Mia reached over to place it in front of her and then turned to the woman's dark-haired companion, who hadn't even bothered to acknowledge her presence. 'And what is it that you will be having, sir?'

'The cappuccino,' he said without looking up from the document he was reading.

'One cappuccino coming up,' Mia said and proceeded to pour it into his lap.

'What the hell…?' Bryn sprang to his feet and tugged the fabric of his trousers away from his lukewarm groin.

'I'm terribly sorry, how very clumsy of me,' she said with no trace of sincerity. 'I'll get you another one straight away.'

'I don't want another one!' He glared down at her and then, narrowing his eyes a fraction, asked, 'Hey, don't I know you?'

She gave him a vacant look and began to turn away. 'Sorry, but I think you must be mistaken. I have never met you before.'

'You're that girl...' he stalled her with a very large, very firm hand on her arm '...the toilet-paper advertisement, right?'

Mia unhinged his fingers and dusted off her arm, shooting him an imperious look. 'I'm sorry, but you must have me mistaken for someone else.'

'I never forget a face and yours is certainly very—'

'*You are fired!*' Tony Pretelli bellowed as he strode towards them. 'Do you hear me, Mia Forrester? F.I.R.E.D. Fired. Now. Right now as of this very minute.'

'Mia Forrester?' Bryn frowned.

'Sorry, Mr Pretelli,' Mia said, momentarily forgetting to employ her Irish accent. 'I didn't mean to do it. It just slipped out of my hands.'

'I saw you, Mia; it didn't just slip out of your hands. You poured it on the poor man! Get your things and leave immediately,' Tony snarled at her and then, turning to Bryn, softened his tone to an obsequious level. 'Please accept my sincere apologies for the appalling behaviour of my staff—er—*ex*-staff member. I will see to it that she personally pays for the damage to your trousers. I'll organise another coffee for you immediately, and can I tempt you with a slice of our house speciality? It's a tiramisu and absolutely delicious—on the house, of course.'

'No, thank you,' Bryn said with a cool little on-off smile.

Typical. Mia gave a little snort. He looks down his nose at everybody. What a pompous jerk.

'But I would like a private word with your—er—ex-staff member,' Bryn added, training his dark blue gaze on her.

Mia's eyes widened in alarm and she started to step backwards. 'But I'm just leaving...'

'Not so fast, Miss Forrester,' he said, capturing her arm once more, his long fingers like a vice around her slim wrist. 'I'm sure your ex-employer won't mind if you humour me for a moment or two.'

Mia looked to Tony for help but he was already on his way back to the kitchen, shouting out another order from table five.

'I think I'll leave you to it,' the brunette woman said to Bryn before sending Mia a pleasant smile. 'I'm Annabelle Heyward, by the way, Miss Forrester. I'm Bryn Dwyer's publicist.'

'Poor you,' Mia muttered not quite under her

breath as she took the older woman's hand with her free one. 'But I'm pleased to meet you. I'm sure you're a very nice person despite the company you keep.'

'Excuse me?' Bryn's dark brows met over his eyes.

'I'll call you later with the latest ratings, Bryn.' Annabelle gave him a little wave as she left the café, her eyes twinkling in amusement.

'Please let go of my arm,' Mia said through clenched teeth. 'Everyone is watching.'

'I don't care who is watching.' He glowered down at her darkly. 'I'd like to know why you think you can get away with tossing a cup of coffee in my lap.'

'I didn't get away with it,' she pointed out with a pert tilt of her chin. 'I got fired, remember?'

'And so you deserved to be. What the hell is the matter with you? What have I ever done to you, for God's sake?'

'How can you ask that?' she spat back, wrenching her arm from his, rubbing at her wrist where his fingers had been. 'Not only have I been fired from here, but I'm also sure I'm going to be dropped from Peach Pie Productions because of what you wrote in this morning's paper. It was my first real live theatre performance and you ruined it. The principal actor was sick and the director asked me to fill in for her and now my career is going to be finished because of you and your stupid opinion, which I'm sure is completely biased and—'

'Oh, *that* Mia Forrester,' he said, rubbing his chin thoughtfully.

Mia stared at him in outrage. What did he mean, *that* Mia Forrester?

'So you got a bad review,' he said dismissively. 'Get over it.'

'Get over it?' She stepped closer and jabbed him in the chest with her index finger. 'How about you get over this? You are the most arrogant, opinionated, chauvinistic smart alec I've ever met. You think you can say whatever you like or indeed write whatever insults you like but I am not going to allow you to get away with it. You have definitely picked the wrong person this time to make fun of. If I lose my understudy job over this, you are going to be very sorry. I will make sure of it.'

Bryn looked down at the little spitfire in front of

him with increasing interest. When was the last
time anyone had told him off, he wondered, really
told him off, no-holds-barred? Most people—particularly women—bowed and scraped to his every
whim, but she was something else again. She was
all flashing grey eyes and swinging blonde pony-
tail, looking more like a schoolgirl than the seductress she'd played so appallingly last night in
Theodore Frankston's new play.

'You should stick to toilet-paper ads,' he said.
'Or have you ever thought about a career change?'

'Have you ever thought about a personality
change?' she tossed back, her eyes like twin
diamonds of sparkling fury.

Bryn suppressed a smile as he let his gaze run
over her lazily. She had a neat figure, very
trimmed and toned, and her skin had a healthy
glow to it as if she was well used to outdoor
activity. She wore no make-up but she had a
fresh-faced beauty that was totally captivating.
He couldn't help thinking she might be just
the type of girl his great-aunt Agnes would
approve of. It would be the perfect solution to
a problem that had been worrying him for quite
some time.

'Listen, Miss Forrester.' He took her to one side out of the way of the hearing of table six. 'I'm sorry you've lost your job here, but really, what's a talented actress like you doing in a place like this?'

She scowled at him. 'You didn't call me talented in your article this morning. You said, and I quote: "A pathetic attempt at portraying a *femme fatale* from a clearly inexperienced actress." Isn't that what you said?'

'It might have run something along those lines.'

'What?' She eyeballed him in fury. 'You don't even remember what you wrote about me?'

'Look.' He dragged a hand through his hair. 'I had a deadline to meet and I'd been out and it was late…'

'Are you telling me you were *drunk* when you wrote that column?'

'Of course not.' He glanced around to make sure no one had heard her fiery accusation. 'Will you keep your voice down? I can do without bad publicity right now.'

Mia straightened to her full height which still left her at a distinct disadvantage to his six-feet-three. 'Do you think I give a damn about your career when you've so cavalierly destroyed mine?'

He compressed his lips for a moment. 'Look, I'll strike a little deal with you.' He took out a business card and handed it to her. 'If you're dropped from the play, give me a call and I'll try and find some other work for you. OK?'

Mia tore the card into tiny pieces and, stepping on her tiptoes, reached to where his top button was undone and stuffed the pieces down his shirt. 'Thanks but no thanks,' she said crisply. 'And I'm going to tell all my friends not to listen to your radio programme ever again. And let me tell you I have a *lot* of friends.'

Bryn watched her flounce back to the kitchen, where, after a short interchange with one of the other waitresses, she scooped up a shoulder bag and left via a rear entrance, her pony-tail still swinging in fury.

He looked down at the neck of his shirt where the sharp little edges were digging into his skin and smiled.

Yes, Great-Aunt Agnes would most definitely approve.

He reached for his mobile and pressed in a few

numbers. 'Annabelle, can you text me Theodore Frankston's number and the name and number of Mia Forrester's current agent?'

'What are you up to, Bryn?' Annabelle's tone was full of suspicion.

He waited until he was outside the café before responding. 'Listen, Annabelle, I've got a plan. You know how you said I needed to improve my image to encourage more female listeners? Well, this is a perfect way to do it.'

Annabelle gave a groan. 'This isn't another one of those publicity stunts that will make me cringe, is it? I really don't think I can cope with the fallout if you get involved with yet another married woman.'

'No, this isn't anything like that. And by the way Summer Riley was divorced, or as good as.'

'She was a slut, Bryn, and for the whole time you were involved with her your ratings slipped to an all-time low. Female listeners fell away in droves and we still haven't got them all back.'

'But that's exactly my point,' Bryn said. 'If I play my cards right with this I could overhaul my image within a matter of days. Think about it. What could be better right now than me having a whirlwind romance with a struggling actress I've just savaged in the Press? Women will love it. It's got that whole love-hate chemistry just like a Hollywood movie.'

'I can't believe I'm hearing this,' Annabelle muttered.

'No, listen, Annabelle,' he insisted. 'Women all over Sydney will tune in to hear how our relationship is going. It's perfect!'

'And how exactly are you going to convince Mia Forrester to have a relationship with you? Last time I looked you were wearing the cappuccino she tossed in your lap,' Annabelle pointed out with more than a hint of dryness.

'I have a strategy in mind that I think will do the trick. Text me those numbers as soon as you track them down. *Ciao.*'

A few minutes later Bryn phoned Theodore Frankston. It was a short conversation and very much to the point.

'It was a rotten review,' Theo growled when Bryn identified himself.

'It was a rotten performance,' Bryn returned. 'That girl was totally wrong for the role. What were you thinking, Theo? You should get rid of her immediately before your reputation is damaged any further.'

'And if I don't?'

'Then on air this afternoon I will warn my listeners to stay away from your play and stay at home and watch TV instead. Your little production company will lose all its sponsors before you can blink.'

'She's not going to like this,' Theo grumbled. 'I like the girl. She's a bit raw but I think with a little more work she'll improve.'

'I like her too,' Bryn said. 'Leave her to me. I've got big plans for her.'

'You're an arrogant bastard,' Theo said. 'Has anyone told you that lately?'

'As a matter of fact they have,' Bryn said with a lazy smile. 'And I liked it so much I can hardly wait until she tells me all over again.'

His phone call to Mia's agent was even more productive. He'd met Roberta Askinthorpe at various social events and although they had flirted occasionally nothing serious had come of it, but he knew she would do anything he asked.

'Long time no hear,' Roberta cooed at him.

'Are you ringing to apologise for that incendiary review you wrote about one of my favourite clients in this morning's paper?'

'Not exactly.'

Roberta laughed. 'No, the Bryn Dwyer I know would never apologise for his actions. What was I thinking?'

'I need you to do something for me, Roberta, but it has to remain a secret.'

'Your wish is my command, you know that, Bryn, darling.'

'I want you to temporarily take Mia Forrester off your books.'

'Why do you want me to do that? She's a real sweetie with bags of potential. I know Theodore's play was a bit out there for her but Sabina was sick at the last minute. Anyway, every actor needs stretching occasionally.'

'I have something else for her to do.'

'But how will I explain it to her?'

'Use my review as an excuse,' he suggested. 'It doesn't have to be permanent. You can take her on again later. I just need her to be without work and representation so she will agree to work for me for the time being.'

'I must say, this sounds very intriguing,' Roberta said. 'Don't tell me you've fallen for the girl?'

Bryn laughed off the suggestion. 'Come on, Roberta, you know me better than that. I'm not the falling-in-love type.'

'Perhaps not, but Mia Forrester is rather a pet,' Roberta pointed out. 'I wouldn't want to see her get hurt. What have you got planned?'

'Stay tuned and you'll find out,' he said. 'But remember this is between you and me.'

'I'll do it but I'm warning you it'll cost you dinner some time.'

'You're on,' he said. 'Dinner it is.'

'In Paris,' she added.

He smiled as he hung up the phone.

CHAPTER TWO

THE telephone started to ring as soon as Mia entered her flat. She stared at it for a moment, wondering if she just ignored it she could put off the inevitable for a little while longer.

'Are you going to get that?' Gina, her flatmate, called out from the bathroom, her voice muffled by the sounds of tooth-brushing.

Mia picked up the phone. 'Mia? Is that you?' her younger sister Ellie's voice sounded in her ear.

'Hi, Ellie. Where are you calling from? Are you still in South America? This line is terrible.'

'I know…' Ellie said, breathing hard. 'Listen, Mia, I'm in trouble. Big trouble.'

Mia felt her insides drop between her knees. 'What's wrong? Where are you? What's happened?'

'I've been arrested.' Ellie let out a little sob.

Mia's eyes widened in shock and her grip on the phone became white-knuckled. '*Arrested! What on earth for?*'

'You know that rainforest-logging protest rally I've been involved with in Brazil? Well, I got arrested and I need bail money wired over to get me out of here.'

'*Oh, my God!*'

'Please don't call Mum and Dad,' Ellie said. 'I don't want to ruin their holiday with Jake and Ashleigh.'

'But we'll have to call them!' Mia insisted.

'No, Mia, please. Dad would have a heart attack on the spot, you know how his doctor told him to take things easy since that last scare.'

'But what about Jake? He'd gladly help out financially. I just know he would.'

'No, Mia. Please don't tell Ashleigh and Jake about this. Ashleigh will be hysterical and it will upset the kids. Promise me you won't tell.'

Mia was all too aware of her sister's fierce pride and had no choice but to reluctantly agree. 'All right, I promise.'

'Thanks, Mia. Just send me some money via my credit card. I've luckily still got that and my passport, although my backpack with my return ticket has been stolen.'

'How much money do you need?'

Ellie told her and Mia's stomach threatened to hit the floor this time. 'I'll send it as soon as I can,' she said. 'It might take me a couple of days to find that kind of money. I have a little in my account but not quite that much.'

'It's all right, I'll manage until you can get it to me,' Ellie said. 'I'm so sorry about this. Please don't tell anyone about it. Not even Gina. I don't want people to worry for nothing. This will all be sorted out in no time and I can't bear the embarrassment of having to explain it all ad nauseam when I get back.'

'What about the Australian Embassy? Should I call them and get them to help?'

'No, just do as I said, Mia,' Ellie said. 'Once that money's in my credit-card account there's a guy here who can help me. It's how things work over here.'

'I'm so worried about you…'

'Don't be, Mia. I'm fine, truly. Look, I've got to go. The guard's making a fuss about the length of the call. I had to bribe him with my last chocolate bar. I'll call you when I'm free. Love you.'

'Love you...' Mia stared at the dead phone, her heart sinking in despair. The amount of money Ellie needed wasn't huge but things had been tight lately and now, with her café job over, if Theodore didn't keep her with the company things could get rather desperate.

The phone rang again while she was still holding it and she answered it to find Theodore on the other end informing her of his decision to drop her from the company. He cut the conversation short as soon as she began to protest.

'Sorry, Mia. My investors are threatening to pull out on the deal after that review. Goodbye.'

She couldn't believe it. Her first foray into live theatre had come to an ignominious end. One bad review and she was back to waiting on tables full-time, except for the fact that, because of this morning's encounter with Bryn Dwyer, she no longer had any tables to wait on. And with Ellie's life in danger thousands of kilometres away she had to have money and fast.

She took a deep, calming breath. *Right, I just have to find another acting job,* she told herself firmly. No matter how small or demeaning it was, she *had* to find work.

She quickly dialled her agent but the conversation, like the one she'd just had with Theodore, was brusque and just as disheartening.

'What's wrong?' Gina asked on her way past a short time later. 'You look like you're about to murder someone.'

'I am,' Mia said, gritting her teeth as she searched for her car keys. 'I'm going to track down the person responsible for making me lose two jobs in one day and tell him exactly what I think of him.'

'You've been dropped from Peach Pie Productions?' Gina's eyes went wide.

Mia tossed one of the sofa cushions aside to retrieve her keys. 'Not just the company but the café as well, and as if that weren't enough my agent just made some pathetic excuse about being too busy to represent me any more. *Grrrrr!*'

'But why?' Gina asked. 'I thought you were brilliant last night, no matter what the review in this morning's paper said.'

'So you saw what he wrote, did you?' Mia asked, scowling furiously. 'God knows who else has seen it and completely written me off as an actor. I can just imagine what everyone is saying. I'm probably the laughing stock of the whole of Sydney by now. No one will ever offer me a role again and as for getting a new agent, who is going to take me on now?'

Gina did her best to be reassuring. 'Try not to worry, Mia, all actors get bad reviews from time to time. It comes with the territory. Maybe a new agent will be a good thing in the long run.'

Mia ground her teeth without answering. Her worries about Ellie made her anger towards Bryn Dwyer escalate to boiling point. He was responsible for this and he was going to pay—big time.

'But why did you lose your job at the café? I thought Tony liked having someone nearly famous working there part-time?'

She gave her flatmate another furious scowl. 'Because I tipped a cup of coffee in a customer's lap, that's why.'

'You mean...' Gina gave her a wide-eyed look '....*on purpose*?'

Mia lifted her head in proud defiance. 'He had it coming to him for writing such a horrible review.'

Gina's eyes nearly popped out of her head. 'You

mean you tipped a cup of coffee in Bryn Dwyer's lap? Bryn Dwyer, the Bachelor of the Year and multimillionaire playboy prince of radio?'

'That's the one.'

'Oh, my God, your career *is* over.'

'Not if I can help it,' Mia said determinedly, jangling her keys in her hand.

Gina gave her a worried look. 'What are you going to do?'

'Like I said—I'm going to see him and tell him exactly what I think of him. He told me to call him if I was dropped from the company, but I'm going to see him in person.'

'Do you think that's such a good idea? He probably has bodyguards or something. He had a stalker before. I remember reading about it in all the magazines. A crazy woman was following him for months, turning up wherever he was, threatening him all the time. His minders might think you're just like her and going to do him some harm.'

Mia gave her a glittering look over her shoulder as she opened the front door to leave. 'I *am* going to do him some harm,' she said. 'And I don't care who tries to stop me. The upsized egotist Bryn Dwyer has finally met his match. You just wait and see.'

The studios of Hot Spot FM were in the leafy suburb of Lane Cove. Mia parked in a side-street and approached the security check-in point. 'I'm here for a live interview with Bryn Dwyer,' she informed the attendant assertively. 'Mia Forrester. I'm an actor.'

The man looked down at his schedule for a moment. 'I'm afraid I don't have you marked down on my sheet. Are you sure your interview is for this afternoon?'

'Yes, I spoke with Mr Dwyer this morning over coffee,' she said and, taking a risk added, 'He asked me to come and see him in person. Perhaps if you could call his studio and check, I'm sure he will verify it for you. We're—er—old friends.'

'Just a second.' The man pressed some numbers and had a brief conversation with the producer before he turned back to her and handed her a security pass through the booth window. 'Here's a security tag.' He activated the boom gate for her and added, 'Go right through,

Miss Forrester; it's studio number five, the third one on the left. The producer will let you know when it's time for your interview. Mr Dwyer's been expecting you.'

Mia walked through with forced casualness while her brain was shooting off in all directions. What did he mean, Mr Dwyer was *expecting* her? How had he known she'd be storming over here to have it out with him?

The two-part studio was where the boom operator had indicated and one of the crew opened the door at her knock and ushered her through. Mia could see Bryn sitting in the transmitting studio next door, his headphones and mouthpiece in place. As if he sensed her presence he swung his chair around and mouthed 'hello' to her, his eyes glinting with something she couldn't quite identify.

She pursed her lips and, although she was seriously tempted to give him a very rude sign with one of her fingers, somehow she resisted the urge and sent him a frosty look instead.

'He's got one more song until the news and weather and then he'll be able to speak to you,' the producer informed her from where he was sitting behind his computer console.

'Thank you,' she said and took the chair he offered.

She could hear the sound of Bryn's deep, mellifluous voice as the show was broadcast around the studio. There was a seven-second delay, which she found a little unnerving because inside the glassed-in section she could see he had stopped speaking to swivel his chair to look at her again.

She gave him another cold look but just then she heard his voice announce his next guest.

'Right after the news and weather I will have with me the utterly gorgeous Mia Forrester, whom I met for the first time this morning when she accidentally spilt a cup of coffee in my lap. Hey, all you out there in radio-land, I'm in *love*.'

Mia's eyes went out on stalks as she sat forward on her chair, her stomach tripping over itself in alarm. What on earth was he doing?

He gave her a quick, confident grin and his voice continued, 'So call me after the news, all you lovers out there in listener-land, and tell me about your most romantic meeting.'

'On air in three minutes,' the producer informed Mia as he flicked another switch on his console.

'But I—' She clamped her mouth shut when

she saw Bryn's lazy smile. *All right*, she thought. I'll do it. I'll go on radio and tell him exactly what I think of him. You just see if I won't.

She was led into Bryn's soundproof studio, fitted with a pair of headphones and seated opposite him in front of a microphone. She could hear the news segment coming to an end and then Bryn smiled as he spoke into his mouthpiece.

'Thank you for joining me in the studio this afternoon, Mia. This is Hot Spot FM and I have with me here the beautiful Mia Forrester, whom I met by accident this morning. And I can tell right my life will never be the same again. I'll take caller number four, who wants to tell us about how she met the love of her life. Hello, Jennifer from way out at Campbelltown. Tell us about your romantic meeting.'

Mia swallowed as a young woman's voice sounded in her ears. 'Hi, Bryn and Mia. I met my husband when he ran into the back of my car at the traffic lights. I was so furious with him but after I'd vented my spleen I suddenly realised how gorgeous he was. He asked me out and the rest, as they say, is history.'

'Thanks, Jennifer, what a great story. Now we

have Andy from Castle Hill on the line. Hi, Andy; how did you meet the love of your life?'

This time a male voice sounded in Mia's ears. 'I met my fiancée when she waxed my legs in preparation for a triathlon I was competing in.'

'No kidding?' Bryn said, winking at Mia. 'So how many waxes did it take to ask her out?'

'Five, but it was worth the pain.'

Bryn laughed. 'Way to go, Andy. Who says men have no sense of romance? Now I think it's Mia's turn to tell you about how she met me this morning. Mia?'

Mia met his dark blue gaze and tightened her mouth. 'I met Bryn Dwyer in the café where up until this morning I was employed part-time. But as a result of my—er—spilling a cup of coffee in his lap I lost my job on the spot and—'

'And lost her heart as well, isn't that right, sweetheart?'

'I—'

'You know the number.' Bryn cut her off as he addressed his listeners. 'Call in and tell us if you agree with the concept of love at first sight.' He took the first caller.

Mia listened with one ear as she tried to make

sense of what was going on. Was this some kind of joke? What the hell was he playing at, pretending he'd fallen in love with her?

The switchboard was buzzing with incoming calls and the producer gave Bryn a thumbs-up sign from the studio next door, his face beaming.

'Now we have Sharon from sunny Seaforth, who has a question for Mia,' Bryn said. 'Go ahead, Sharon.'

'Mia, did you feel an instant attraction for Bryn or did it take a few minutes before you realised you were falling in love with him?'

'I...' Mia caught the gleam in Bryn's dark gaze and sent him a blistering glare. 'No, not instantly...it was more of a slow realisation that here was a man who would stop at nothing to get his way and—'

'See how well she knows me already?' Bryn cut her off again. 'How about a question from Corinne? Go ahead, Corinne.'

'Mia, I was wondering if you are worried about falling in love with one of Sydney's notorious playboys. What if he lets you down?'

'I don't think he'll let me down,' Mia said, finally catching on and hatching a vengeful little plot of her own. She gave Bryn a beguiling smile and added, 'Not now that we're planning to get married as soon as possible. He proposed to me this morning and I said yes.'

Within seconds the switchboard was jammed with calls and the producer gave the signal for the next bracket of music to be played.

Mia waited until she was sure they were off air. 'What the hell do you think you're doing? I'm not in love with you!'

'I know,' Bryn said, leaning back in his chair to survey her outraged features. 'But the listeners don't know that and neither does my producer.'

'You mean…' she glanced at the still beaming producer in the studio next door and then back at Bryn '…you mean they think it's…*real*?'

'Of course they think it's real.'

'Are you crazy or something?'

'Not crazy, just hungry for more ratings.' A segment of advertisements began to play as he continued, 'I thought since you ruined a pair of Armani trousers this morning the very least you could do was give my ratings a boost by pretending to be in love with me for a week or two.' He pressed another button. 'But that bit about marriage was total overkill. It'll be all over the papers tomorrow.'

Mia felt her heart give an extra beat. 'The papers?'

'Yep. Journalists love this sort of stuff. Celebrity playboy meets perfect match.' He smiled a white-toothed smile. 'But we can go along with it for a while. What do you think?'

'I think you're a jerk, that's what I think. I lost my job because of you.'

'I told you you're wasted in the café; you could do much better than that.'

'Not the café, although that was bad enough,' she bit out through clenched teeth. 'I was dropped from Peach Pie Productions this morning. Theodore Frankston saw your review and decided to pull me out completely. Then I spoke to my agent who told me she was too busy to represent me properly but I know it was because of your stupid review.'

'Too bad.'

'It's worse than bad. I have bills to pay.' *And I need a heck of a lot of money to get my sister out of trouble*, she wanted to insert but stopped herself just in time. 'I've not long moved into a flat with a friend. How am I going to meet my commitments when I no longer have a job and no agent to find me a new one?'

'Ah, but you do have a job,' he said. 'I just gave you one.'

She frowned at him in confusion. 'What are you talking about?'

He leaned forward in his chair until his knees were almost touching hers. Mia hadn't realised how very dark his eyes were until that moment and she felt her tummy do a funny little moth-like flutter as she was pulled into their deep, ocean-blue depths.

'I want you to act the role of my devoted fiancée,' he said. 'I would have settled for girl-friend but, since you mentioned the M word in front of two-point-four million listeners, I'm afraid we'll have to run with that role instead.'

'*Your fiancée?*' She gasped. '*You want me to pretend to be your fiancée?*'

He flicked a glance at the monitor and pressed another button before he sat back in his seat. 'You're an actor, right?'

She gave him a resentful look. 'Yes, but according to this morning's paper not a very good one.'

'Here's your chance to prove me wrong,' he said. 'If you can convince the Press and my listeners that you are indeed in love with me then I'll take back everything I said. I'll pay you, of course. What was Frankston's company giving you?'

She told him and he gave a snort. 'What a joke. No wonder you didn't put your heart into that role. I'll pay you four times that much, plus expenses.'

'Expenses?'

'Hang on a minute.' He turned his headphones back on and began to speak on air. 'You heard it first on Hot Spot FM. Bryn Dwyer the confirmed bachelor is in love with a little lady who has promised to be his wife. You know the number. Give me a call to congratulate me. This is one very happy man.'

Mia sat silently fuming. This was getting ridiculous. Surely he didn't expect her to take him seriously?

She chewed her lip for a moment.

It *was* a lot of money he was offering. Besides, it might only be for a week or two, maybe a couple of months at the most. And it would certainly solve Ellie's problems, which was her biggest priority right now. And she was an actor, so it shouldn't be a problem playing the role, but still…

She stole a covert look at him as he chatted with another caller. He was smiling, which made his eyes crinkle up at the edges in a rather attractive way.

'So what do you say?' he said as he went off air again.

'What if I don't agree to this?' she said, not wanting to feed his ego by sounding too keen.

He shifted his lips from side to side as if he was thinking about a suitable plan of action. Mia felt distinctly uneasy. She felt as if she was now under his control and she didn't like it one little bit. She had come storming to the studio to tell him what she thought of him but somehow he had turned the tables on her.

'There were witnesses to your assault on my person this morning,' he said into the little silence. 'And, like you, I have a lot of friends, several of them with impressive law degrees. All it would take is one phone call and you could be in very hot water, even hotter than the liquid you tossed in my lap.'

Mia's throat moved up and down. Surely he

wouldn't press charges if she didn't fall in with his plans?

She met his midnight-blue eyes and swallowed again,

Yes. He would.

She lowered her gaze. 'You mentioned something about expenses…'

'Yes. You'll need to have nice clothes and get your hair done occasionally. I don't expect you to pay for that out of your own pocket. I'll make sure you have a substantial clothing and grooming allowance. So have we got a deal?'

'How long do you expect me to play this role for you?'

'Not long; a week or two, maybe longer.'

She narrowed her eyes at him. 'How much longer?'

'What say we give it a month at the most and then we'll call it off?'

'What will happen to your ratings then?'

He gave her another grin. 'They'll probably increase due to my heartbroken state. Everyone will feel sorry for me being dumped.'

Mia rolled her eyes.

'I'm off air in thirty minutes,' he said, flicking

another switch. 'Wait for me in the cafeteria and we'll go somewhere where we can have another chat about the deal. But in the meantime, don't let the cat out of the bag. I don't want anyone at the studio to suspect this is a stunt.'

'What about your publicist?'

'I'll tell her only what she needs to hear but no one else is to know, not even your family and friends.'

'I can't lie to my family and friends!'

'You're not lying, Mia. You're acting. There's a difference.'

She opened her mouth but he went back on air before she could get a single word of protest out. She blew out a breath of frustration and, snatching up her bag, made her way to the cafeteria she'd seen on her way in.

CHAPTER THREE

MIA was almost relieved when Bryn finally joined her half an hour later. She'd been practically besieged by staff rushing up to congratulate her on her impending marriage to Sydney's crown prince of the airwaves.

'Sorry about that,' he said as he led her to an office down the hall. He smiled at her as he pushed open the door marked with his name. 'See what a sensation you've caused?'

'*I've* caused?' Mia swung around to glare at him once they were alone inside. 'If you hadn't rubbished me the way you did none of this would have happened.'

'You were the one who told everyone we were engaged,' he pointed out.

'I only did that to get back at you for saying we'd fallen in love this morning.' She gave him a disparaging glare and added, 'As if I'd ever fall in love with someone like you.'

'I don't know why you're so upset,' he said. 'Your season with Theodore would have ended in two weeks anyway—then what were you going to do? Wait on tables until something else turned up? I'm doing you a favour, Mia. I'm giving you the sort of exposure most wannabe actors would give a right arm for. Your face will be on every national paper tomorrow. The Press will want interviews, magazines will carry your picture on their covers and before you know it every film or theatre producer in town will be begging you to audition for them. You'll have agents falling over themselves to represent you.'

Mia frowned as she thought about it. It certainly would get her name out there, but at what cost? How would she ever explain it to her family?

'I don't like the idea of being used as a marketing ploy, especially without consultation with me first,' she said. 'And I don't appreciate being blackmailed.'

'Yes, well, I don't appreciate having my groin soaked with hot coffee,' he returned with a glint in his eyes.

Mia's eyes went to his groin. He was leaning against his desk, his long legs outstretched, the fabric of his trousers pulled tight over his…

She wrenched her gaze away and forced herself to meet his laughing blue eyes. 'I'm sure no permanent damage was done and even if it was I'm sure the rest would do you good. It's a wonder it hasn't dropped off by now from overuse.'

'Maybe you should check it out just to make sure it's still on active service,' he suggested with a lift of an eyebrow.

She gave him a withering look and folded her arms across her chest. 'I don't think so.'

He laughed and pushed himself away from the desk to stand right in front of her. He tipped up her chin with one long finger and looked into her eyes. 'You've got such an expressive little face. I can't stop looking at you. Those big grey eyes of yours remind me of a stormy afternoon sky, one minute dark and brooding, the next flashing with lightning sparks of fury.'

Mia held her breath as he began to trace his thumb across her bottom lip, back and forth, back and forth until she could feel her mouth tingling. She knew she should have at least made a token effort to move out of his reach but somehow his touch was totally mesmerising. Her heart began to hammer behind her chest as he placed his hand on her hip and brought her even closer.

'Wh-what are you doing?' she croaked.

He held her firm, his long fingers splayed over the slim curve of her hip, his mouth tilted in a little smile. 'I thought we should get this bit over with in private. That way when we have to do it in public it won't feel so strange. It's like a rehearsal, if you like.'

'A rehearsal?' She gave a quick nervous swallow. 'A rehearsal for what?'

His head came down, hovering just above hers, his warm, hint-of-mint breath brushing over her lips as he said in a deep, spine-tingling voice, 'We need to rehearse the kiss scenes we'll be expected to play in public.'

Her stomach gave an unexpected lurch. 'K-kiss scenes?'

His mouth moved a little closer, his chest so close now she could feel the deep rumble of his voice against her breasts when he spoke. 'Yes, you know—where I put my mouth on yours and you kiss me back.'

'I know what a kiss scene is but I—' Mia began but before she could get the full sentence out, his mouth had come down and settled firmly on hers.

It was a shock to feel his lips moving over hers so persuasively. She'd had every intention of fighting him but somehow as soon as those firm, warm lips connected with hers she felt an electric charge rush through her as if some sort of visceral energy was passing from his body to hers. Before she knew it she was responding to him, her mouth opening at the first sweep of his tongue. He entered her mouth with a toe-curling thrust that sent a riot of sensations through her body from her breasts to her thighs. It was madness but she just couldn't help it. She kept reminding herself how much she hated him but what she was feeling in his arms took over the rational, cool-headed, thinking part of her brain. Every part of her body reacted to him. She could feel the prickling tension in her breasts as he brought her even harder up against his chest and deepened the kiss. She could even feel her inner thighs quivering at the thought of what was pressing so insistently just above them. She had never been so thoroughly kissed in her entire life and this was just a rehearsal! God knew how she would cope with the real thing.

But none of this is real, she told herself sternly. It's an act, a publicity stunt for him to increase his ratings. It has nothing to do with reality, nothing to do with real feelings and responses.

It was an act.

Bryn lifted his head and looked down at her flushed features. 'Wow, I think I might have to take back everything I said in my column. That was an Oscar-winning performance. No one would ever think you weren't in love with me after that.'

Mia eased herself out of his hold, her eyes flashing with rage. 'If you think I'm going to be manhandled by you whenever you feel like it then you're in for a big shock.'

'It's only a performance, just like any other,' he said. 'Besides, you kissed the leading man last night, not very convincingly in my opinion, but then maybe he had bad breath or something.'

'He did not have bad breath.'

'Then what was the problem? Didn't you like the guy?'

'Actors don't have to like the person they're playing opposite, which is just as well, as I can't think of a person I hate more than you.'

'What a professional challenge this will be for you, then,' he observed with a mocking smile playing about his mouth. 'Convincing the public you're in love with me when all the time you really hate my guts.'

'I can do it,' she bit out with pride-fuelled determination. 'I'll show you I'm not the inexperienced, pathetic actor you apparently think I am.'

'Good,' he said. 'We'll start with public performance number one this evening. I'll send a car for you at seven. Wear something glamorous and sexy.'

'I don't have anything glamorous and sexy.'

He reached for his wallet and, opening it, peeled off a thick wad of notes and handed it to her. 'Buy something.'

Mia stared at the money without touching it.

'Go on,' he said. 'It's part of the deal, remember?'

'I don't want your disgusting money. I'd rather wear rags than take anything off you.'

He tugged her towards him and with a deftness that left her completely breathless he tucked the wad of notes down the front of her cotton top right between her heaving breasts.

'When I say go and buy something sexy and glamorous I mean it, Mia. Got that? You're playing a role for me and I expect and indeed am paying you to give a brilliant performance.'

Mia gave him a fulminating glare as she retrieved the money out of her top and stuffed it in the back pocket of her jeans. 'I might have to act my heart out in public but when we're alone I'm still going to hate you with every bone in my body. Got that?'

'Loud and clear,' he said, holding the door open for her. 'Come on, I'll walk you to your car.'

'I can find my own way.' She made to brush past but he put out an arm to stop her. She jerked back from the feel of his muscled arm against the softness of her breasts.

Her eyes locked with his and her heart gave an extra beat at the diamond-sharp glitter in his dark gaze.

'Don't fight me, Mia, because when I fight, I fight dirty. You'd be wise to remember that.'

'Tell me something I don't already know,' she tossed back. 'You're an unscrupulous playboy with nothing better to do with your time than manipulate people to do what you want. How pathetic.'

'I'll tell you what's pathetic,' he said, a thread of anger beginning to tighten his voice. 'Your little attempt at pay-back this morning was a childish impulse that clearly demonstrates how ill-suited you are for anything other than those ridiculous toilet-paper ads you've done in the past.'

Mia clenched her fists by her sides. 'Why don't you just go ahead and sue me? Go on. I dare you.'

'Don't tempt me, little lady. How long do you think it would take you to find another job if I tell the truth about what really happened this morning? There isn't an agent who would take you on and you damn well know it. You reputation as a hot-headed little prima donna would make anyone think twice about representing you.'

Mia tried to outstare him but something about the rigid set of his jaw warned her against pitting her puny strength against his. He was a man used to having things his way and anyone in the way would be ruthlessly disposed of with whatever means he had available. She knew she would never find work in the industry again if he put his mind to it. He had connections and in the acting world that meant everything. One bad word and her reputation would be ruined. One bad review was enough. How much worse would it be if he took it into his mind to totally alienate her future career prospects?

She lowered her eyes and though it irked her intolerably she made no demur as he took her hand and led her out of his office through the building and the grounds until they came to her car.

'See you tonight,' he said, stepping back from the car as she started the engine.

'See you in hell,' she muttered darkly as she backed out.

Bryn watched her roar away in a clang of clutch and gears, her smooth cheeks still bright pink with outraged colour.

Once she was out of sight he ran his tongue over his lips. He could still taste the summer-strawberry flavour of her soft mouth where it had been pressed against his. Even his chest felt as if she were still up against it, her slender curves fitting so neatly against him as if she were tailor-made for him. Holding her close had triggered a deep pulse of desire that even now he could feel thudding insistently in his blood. He couldn't remember a time when he'd felt so turned on by a woman.

He gave himself a mental shake. He didn't believe in love at first sight. He didn't believe in romantic love at all. The term 'love' was all too often used when the word 'lust' would have been much more appropriate. Lust at first sight; now, there was a concept he could get his head around.

He was *in lust* with Mia Forrester.

That was more like it.

Lust he could handle.

But even so, a tiny frown closed the distance between his eyebrows as he turned and walked back to the studio building.

CHAPTER FOUR

'OH, MY God, is it true?' Gina gasped as soon as Mia walked through the door of their tiny flat in Neutral Bay. 'I listened to you on the radio. Are you *really* engaged to him?'

'Um...well...you know...I...it...we...'

'It's just *soooo* romantic!' Gina gushed. 'I thought you hated him and now you're going to be married. Talk about a whirlwind affair. Can I be bridesmaid?'

'I'm not...sure what plans we will be making about that just yet,' Mia said, hating Bryn all over again for making her lie to her closest friend. 'It's all happened so fast. My feet haven't touched the ground yet.'

'How did it happen? I mean, did you just suddenly realise he was the man of your dreams? Was it truly love at first sight?'

Mia had to dig deeply into her acting repertoire to sound anywhere near convincing. 'I went there to tell him what I thought of him but as soon as I saw him sitting there...I couldn't control my reaction. It was...unbelievable.'

'God, I wish some gorgeous guy would sweep me off my feet like that,' Gina said. 'And think of how rich and famous he is. You'll never have to worry about the rent again.'

'His money doesn't matter to me in the slightest,' Mia lied.

The truth was, Bryn Dwyer's money was the only reason she was doing this, to help Ellie, otherwise she would have told him exactly where to put his stupid fiancée role with considerable relish. She'd already deposited the wad of money he'd given her into her sister's credit-card account, which had in some way made her feel a little less compromised about what she was doing in playing the role he'd assigned her. At least it would tide her sister over until she could get her hands on some more.

'I'm sure his money doesn't matter to you but every little bit helps,' Gina responded pragmatically. 'So when are you seeing him again?'

Mia glanced at her watch and felt her stomach clench in panic at how she was going to be ready in time. 'In about two hours.'

'Two hours?' Gina looked aghast. 'But you haven't even done your hair!'

'Can I borrow that black evening dress of yours?' Mia asked as she kicked off her shoes and released her pony-tail.

'Which one? The one with the diamanté halter-neck or the one with the split up the thigh?'

'Which do you think is sexier?'

Gina scrunched her face up as she thought about it. 'Definitely the split—besides, you've got the legs for it.'

Mia stared at her reflection an hour and forty-five minutes later. There was no trace of the struggling and out-of-work actor now. In her place was a sophisticated vision in close-fitting black satin, her blonde hair scooped up in a casual but still elegant twist on top of her head, the glittering drop earrings she'd borrowed off Gina giving the final touch of glamour.

'Wow…you look fabulous. Bryn is going to

fall in love with you all over again when he sees you,' Gina said.

Mia stifled a cynical little laugh. Bryn Dwyer didn't seem to be the type to fall in love with anybody but himself. The Press had been full of his numerous relationships, none of them lasting more than a week or two. And no wonder, she thought uncharitably. With his ego the size it was, there wouldn't be room for anyone else's in any of his relationships.

'That's him!' Gina whispered as the doorbell sounded. She scooped up the evening bag she'd lent Mia and ushered her towards the door.

Mia flicked a loose tendril out of her eye and opened the door to find a man dressed in a chauffeur's uniform standing there.

'Good evening, Miss Forrester. My name is Henry. I'm Mr Dwyer's driver. I have been instructed to take you to him for this evening's event. He had another commitment but told me to tell you he will meet you there.'

Mia saw Gina's eyes go out on stalks but she herself was not so impressed by such opulent wealth. She hated unnecessary displays of prosperity and couldn't help feeling Bryn had done it deliberately to remind her of his power over her. She inwardly fumed as she wondered what his other commitment had been—no doubt a quick dalliance with one of his numerous lovers.

She gave the driver a pleasant smile and followed him out to the stretch limousine and turned around in her seat to give the awestruck Gina a little fingertip wave once Henry had settled her inside.

A few minutes later they were travelling across the Harbour Bridge into the city, the summer sun still high in the sky, casting a golden glow over the high-rise buildings. There were numerous yachts out, their white sails in perfect accord with the sail-like structure of the Sydney Opera House, which sparkled in the bright sunshine.

Within a short time Henry drove into the sweeping driveway of one of the premier hotels, where a host of paparazzi were already gathered in anticipation as one of the hotel staff stepped forward to open her door.

Mia had to rely on what she'd learnt in a role play workshop she'd done a few months back. She stepped out of the vehicle as if she were royalty, smiling graciously for the flashing cameras as she made her way across the red carpet to the ostentatious foyer.

The ceiling was dripping with crystal chandeliers, the marbled floor beneath her high-heeled feet was polished to perfection and huge, fragrant floral arrangements dominated the centre table in front of the grand, sweeping staircase.

A journalist thrust a microphone in her face. 'Miss Forrester, tell us how it feels to have won the heart of Sydney's most confirmed bachelor.'

She smiled sweetly and answered in a breathy tone. 'It feels absolutely wonderful.'

'You are the envy of the young and single female population of Sydney,' another one said. 'No one ever thought he would commit. Can you tell us your secret?'

'There is no secret about love,' she said. 'It takes you by surprise when you're least expecting it.'

'Is it true you met by accident?' a female reporter asked.

'Yes…' Mia gave a coy smile. 'I accidentally spilt a cup of coffee in his lap.'

'Is there any truth in the rumour that Mr Dwyer's comments in this morning's paper in regard to your performance in Theodore Frankston's latest production precipitated your—er—little accident?'

'No, of course not…as I said, it was an accident. It just slipped out of my hand,' Mia lied with increasing confidence. 'It was only when he stood up that I realised who he was and…well…I was overwhelmed by my feelings, as indeed he was too.'

'There has been some suggestion that this is all a publicity stunt,' another journalist said. 'Do you have any comment to make?'

'Yes.' She looked towards the television camera, giving her lashes a little flutter before she continued in the same breathy tone. 'I would like to say to all those sceptics out there that there is such a thing as love at first sight. Bryn and I are living proof of it. As soon as we met it was like…kismet.' She was on a roll and continued with a hand pressed to her bosom. 'I could almost hear the angels singing.' She gave a dreamy sigh. 'I can't wait until we're married. It's like a dream come true.'

'Er—thank you, Miss Forrester.' The journalist turned to the camera. 'Well, you've heard it straight from the filly's mouth, so to speak. To those who've just tuned in, Sydney's twice-in-a-row Bachelor of the Year has finally met his match. The official engagement of Miss Mia Forrester and Mr Bryn Dwyer has made headlines around the country.'

Mia turned as a hand touched her on the elbow.

'This way, Miss Forrester,' a hotel staff member said as he directed her towards the staircase. 'Mr Dwyer will be here shortly. The ballroom is on the first floor.'

Mia picked up the tiny train on her dress and glided up the stairs as the cameras flashed behind her. It occurred to her then that she was quite enjoying herself. She hadn't expected to but somehow she was relishing the role of Bryn's fiancée. She was particularly pleased with her portrayal of a star-struck *ingénue*. Who said she couldn't act?

The ballroom was decked out with pink and blue balloons and streamers, the arc of tables beautifully and elegantly set for dinner around a small dance floor.

The other guests had already assembled and were enjoying their pre-dinner drinks as the waiters began to lead them to their tables.

'You're on table one,' the same staff member informed her. 'Come this way.'

Mia followed him to the table where some of the guests were already seated. They sprang to their feet as she approached and congratulated her effusively.

'Such wonderful news!'

'I always knew he'd do it some day.'

'But you're gorgeous! No wonder he was instantly smitten.'

Mia lapped it up. She felt like a Hollywood movie star. She smiled and took each hand in turn, doing her best to memorise names and faces as each person introduced themselves.

'Here, sit next to me.' An older woman called Jocey Myers patted the seat beside her. 'Bryn will be here soon.'

'Thank you.' Mia sat down and settled her gown around her.

'He's probably visiting his great-aunt,' Jocey said in an undertone. 'Has he told you about her?'

Mia wasn't sure how to answer. She was

supposed to be his fiancée. Surely a fiancée would know just about everything about the man she was about to marry. 'Um...yes...'

'She's not expected to live much longer, poor dear,' Jocey went on. 'He doesn't know I know. I only found out by accident, as my mother-in-law is in the same palliative-care unit.' She leaned towards Mia conspiratorially. 'No one at the station knows, of course; it just wouldn't go with the image, now, would it?'

'Er—no...'

Mia frowned as she took in the information about Bryn's relative. She felt as if she'd done him a disservice, assuming he'd been off with one of his lovers when instead he had been sitting by the bedside of a terminally ill relative.

She thought of her own elderly relatives, the extended family that she so adored, uncles and aunts, great-uncles and great-aunts and her three remaining grandparents. They had filled her life with such amazing love and security and given true meaning to the word family.

Jocey tapped her on the shoulder. 'Ah. here he is now.'

Mia turned to see Bryn approach the table, his

tall, commanding stance turning every head in the room. He bent down and, before she could do anything to counteract it, pressed a lingering kiss to her mouth.

'How's my beautiful fiancée this evening?'

She gave him a tight smile without answering, but she sent him a message with her eyes which she hoped no one else could see.

His mouth tilted as he tapped her gently on the tip of her nose with the end of one long finger. 'I can see you're speechless with love for me. How adorably sweet.'

'You lucky dog.' One of the older men thumped Bryn on the shoulder on his way past to the drinks waiter.

'I told you it would happen eventually,' another guest said.

'I thoroughly approve,' one of the other women said. 'You should have seen how she handled the media. A natural, if you ask me.'

'How *did* you handle the media?' Bryn asked softly as he sat down beside her.

Mia couldn't help feeling a little ashamed of her earlier behaviour with the Press. She'd come across as an empty-headed, star-struck bimbo. If only she'd known he was visiting his dying relative. Now she just felt silly and childish.

'It was a piece of cake,' she whispered back.

'Good girl,' he said and reached for his glass. 'I'd hate for this children's charity to be spoilt by a bad Press release.'

Mia stiffened in her seat. *Children's charity?* She glanced towards the podium, where a brightly festooned sign portrayed the emblem of the charity for kids with cancer. Bryn's name was printed there as principle sponsor and another wave of shame passed through her from head to toe.

'What's wrong?' he asked. 'You look a little flustered.'

Mia bent her head and stared at her cutlery. 'I'm not the least bit flustered.'

'Why are you blushing?'

'I'm not blushing,' she denied even as her face felt as if it was going to explode with heat. 'It's hot in here.'

'Let's go get some air,' he said and drew her to her feet.

She had no choice but to go with him. The other guests looked on indulgently as he escorted her from the ballroom, a couple of cameras flashing at them as they went past.

He waited until he'd led her into a quiet alcove out of the way of the Press. 'I'm sorry I was late. I had something to see to.'

'Why didn't you tell me you were visiting your great-aunt?'

He frowned down at her, his dark eyes narrowing into slits. 'Who told you about my great-aunt?'

'Jocey Myers.'

His features darkened and Mia noticed his hands begin to clench by his sides. 'She had no right to do that.'

'I think she had the right to tell me the important details of your life and background,' she said. 'I can't act this role if I don't know who the other principle character is.'

'You don't need to know me. This is all an act. Just run with the script I gave you.'

'The script you gave me has some very big gaps in it,' she said. 'I can't do this convincingly if I don't know who you are as a person. No one will believe I have fallen in love with you unless I can prove I know who you really are.'

Bryn thought about it for a moment. 'All right,

I'll fill you in on some details but they are to go no further. Understood?'

She nodded.

'Right, then.' He took a breath and wondered where to start. 'My parents were killed when I was seven. I hardly remember what they looked like now. My great-aunt Agnes stepped in and brought me up. End of story.'

Mia frowned. 'But surely—'

'I don't remember, OK?' His eyes hardened as they lasered hers. 'Now let's go back and do what we're here to do.'

'What exactly are we here to do?' she asked as she trotted to keep up with his long strides.

'We're here to raise a hundred thousand dollars for the Children's Cancer Ward at St Patrick's.'

She stared at his back as he started back towards the ballroom. 'Wait!' She tugged on his arm and he turned to face her. 'What do you want me to do?'

He looked down at her mouth for a moment before he tore his gaze away. 'I told you this afternoon. I want you to act the role of the devoted fiancée. Did you happen to cover that at stage school?'

She lifted her chin. 'That was in Tricky Relationships 101.'

He threw back his head and laughed.

'What's so funny?' she asked. 'You don't think I can do tricky relationships?'

He placed a casual arm around her shoulders as he led her back into the ballroom. 'I'm beginning to think I've seriously underestimated your acting ability.'

'I told you I can act,' she said through a forced smile as someone stopped to take their photo.

'So you did but up until today I hadn't seen you do it very convincingly.'

'I was going on instinct rather than experience in Theo's play. I just needed more time to get my head around the role. I was the understudy, remember,' she said.

He stopped in his tracks to look down at her, a small frown beetling his brows. 'So what you're saying is you've never actually been in love?'

'Um…no…' She shifted her gaze. 'I've had a few close calls but nothing very serious.'

'Have you lived with anyone before?'

'No…'

'Been engaged before?'

She rolled her eyes at him. 'No, of course not. In case it has escaped your notice, most women these days prefer to be in love with the man they've agreed to marry.'

He gave her a thoughtful look that seemed to go on and on for endless seconds, his dark blue eyes steady on hers.

Mia began to brace herself for his next question. Here it comes, she thought.

The big one.

Have You Slept With Anyone Before?

'I think you'll enjoy the rest of the evening,' he finally said. 'Do you like dancing?'

It wasn't the question she'd been expecting and it took her a moment to register what he'd asked. 'Oh, yes...I love dancing...'

Bryn glanced down at her when she wasn't looking his way. She had dressed beautifully for the evening, the clinging black satin showing off every toned curve of her slight frame. Her bright and intelligent grey eyes were highlighted by a smoky eye-shadow and eyeliner and her soft mouth glistened with a camellia-pink lip-gloss.

There was an ingenuous air about her he found incredibly alluring. So many women he'd been involved with in the past had been so street-smart and worldly he'd found it grating after a while. He knew his money and status had been the draw card in such relationships, but Mia had no interest in him either as a person or for what he could give her in terms of money or prestige. She was with him under sufferance and he knew as soon as they were alone again she would take the very first opportunity to remind him of it.

His gut gave a tiny twinge of guilt as he thought of the conversation he'd had with his great-aunt earlier that evening. He'd hated lying to the one person who had stood by him all of his life, but it had been worth it to see the sheer joy on her pain-ravaged face as he'd confirmed his engagement. He wasn't sure if she would believe him at first but somehow she had. He'd told her as soon as he'd met Mia he'd found the woman of his dreams. It was after all more or less the truth. Mia Forrester was exactly the stuff male dreams were made of.

'Oh, my darling boy!' Agnes had clutched his hand in both of her frail ones in delight. 'I'm so pleased. At first I thought it must have been a publicity stunt or a way to get me to change my will. I know you weren't happy about my conditions but I couldn't risk you throwing yourself away on someone who was only after you for your money. And, besides, your parents wouldn't have wanted you to be this bitter for so long.'

Bryn inwardly grimaced at the thought of how his great-aunt's will was written. It was a lot of money, not that he needed it personally, of course, but he wasn't going to stand by and see the person responsible for his parents' death inherit the lot. That was taking forgiveness way too far.

'You're exactly like your father,' his great-aunt continued. 'He fell in love with your mother the very first time he met her. It was so romantic.' She gave a heartfelt sigh and added, 'I have dreamed of this moment. I have wanted this for you for so long, for you to settle down with a nice girl instead of those money-hungry ones you usually date. I heard her on the radio with you this afternoon— she sounds so sweet. When can I meet her?'

'I'll bring her to see you tomorrow,' he found himself promising, hoping his acting fiancée would agree to it.

'That would be wonderful; I can hardly wait to see her. I'm sure she's absolutely perfect for you.'

Bryn bent down and kissed her papery cheek as he made to leave. 'Yes,' he said, a funny flutter coming and going in his chest as he brought Mia Forrester's feisty little heart-shaped face to mind. 'She is perfect. Absolutely perfect.'

The first course was being served as they came back into the ballroom. Mia sat down with considerable relief when Bryn's arm slipped from around her shoulders as he turned to speak to the person on his right. Having him so physically close was deeply unsettling, for ever since he'd kissed her that afternoon her awareness of him had lifted to an almost intolerable level. All her senses were finely tuned to pick up on his every movement or gesture. When she turned her head towards her left shoulder she could even smell his cologne on her skin where his arm had lain. She knew she'd have to get used to having him touch her in public but each time he did so she felt as if another part of her was being made more vulnerable to him.

She reached for her wine glass and felt his leg brush against hers. She tried to edge away but his hand came down on the middle of her thigh. The weight of his fingers felt like a scorch through the thin fabric of her gown. And her heart began to pick up its pace when he turned to speak to her, his dark blue eyes steady on hers.

'Everything all right, sweetheart?'

'F-fine…just fine…' She moistened her lips and forced herself not to flinch away when his hand moved upwards a fraction.

He leaned closer to whisper in her ear, 'Relax.'

'I am relaxed.'

'No, you're not. You're as tense as a trip-wire.'

'Only because your hand is where it shouldn't be,' she said, smiling inanely as someone took their photo.

'I'm your fiancé. I'm supposed to touch you.'

'In public—yes.'

'This is in public. In fact, it couldn't be more public. There are at least five hundred people in this room.'

'It's not public under the table,' Mia pointed out tightly.

He gave her a lazy smile and took his hand off her thigh to place it on the nape of her neck, his long, warm fingers toying with the silky tendrils of her hair. 'Is that better?'

A shiver of reaction passed right through her from the top of her head to her toes. She forced herself to maintain eye contact, knowing that people were watching, but it was increasingly difficult to disguise her reaction to him. She hoped he would assume she was simply acting but something about his smile suggested he was well aware of the effect he was having on her.

'Let's dance,' he suggested after a little silence.

Mia was glad of an excuse to move out of his embrace, but it wasn't until she was on the dance floor with his arms pulling her into his rock-hard body that she realised she had just stepped out of a sizzling frying-pan and straight into the leaping flames of a fire she had no hope of controlling.

There wasn't even room for air between their bodies as he turned her into a quick-stepping waltz. She was pressed to him from chest to thigh, the thin, close-fitting fabric of her gown no barrier to the searing heat of his body. Her breasts were pushed up against him and he took full advantage of it by dipping his gaze over their creamy curves.

Mia felt her skin tingle from the burning heat in his eyes, and her stomach did a nervous little flip turn when she felt the unmistakable evidence of his growing erection against her belly.

'Maybe this wasn't such a good idea…' she said, trying not to blush but knowing she was failing miserably.

'Why?' He skilfully turned her in his arms and brought her even closer. 'I'm enjoying myself.'

She gave him a caustic look while her back was turned to the tables. 'No doubt you are but let me tell you I am not.'

'I thought you said you liked dancing?'

'This is not dancing, this is making out in front of an audience!' she hissed back.

'You want to go somewhere more private?'

'I don't want to go anywhere with you.'

'Careful, Mia, there are cameras everywhere. We have a deal, remember? Now, stop looking at me as if you're going to take me apart piece by piece and kiss me instead.'

She gave him a recalcitrant look. 'I am not going to kiss you.'

His dark eyes held hers challengingly. 'Yes you are.'

She elevated her chin defiantly. 'Make me. I dare you.'

'It will be my pleasure,' he said and tugging her up hard against him brought his mouth down on hers.

CHAPTER FIVE

MIA was determined not to respond to his kiss but her awareness of the rest of the guests watching made it difficult for her to put her resistance into action. She began to kiss him back and told herself she'd had no other choice, but another part of her wondered if she would have responded anyway, audience or not.

His kiss softened and she felt herself being carried away by the swell of passion his searching tongue evoked as it entered the warm, moist cave of her mouth. She heard her soft sigh mingle with his and something hot and liquid seemed to burst deep inside her, running through her in a flowing tide that melted her to the core. Her chest was thrumming with a build-up of unfamiliar emotion, an acute neediness she had never experienced before. It frightened her at the same time as it intrigued her. How could someone she hated so much provoke such intense reactions in her body? Had she no control over her responses to him? Was it lust or something much more dangerous?

Bryn stepped back from her and looked down at her flushed face for a long moment, seemingly unaware that the band was still halfway through a song. Other couples were dancing around them but Mia felt as if time had come to a halt right where they were standing facing each other. She ran her tongue over her lips and her chest fluttered again when she saw his eyes dip to her mouth, lingering there for several pulsing seconds.

'We should get back to the table,' he said, his eyes dark and unreadable when they slowly came back to hers.

'Yes…yes…we should…'

He took her arm and, sliding his hand down its slender length, curled his fingers around hers and led her back without another word.

The rest of the meal passed without incident, although Mia felt as if her face was going to crack from smiling all the time. Guest after guest

approached her to congratulate her on taming
the wild heart of Bryn Dwyer, and, while she
thanked them each in turn, she found by the end
of the evening she was totally exhausted by the
pretence. It seemed wrong to be deliberately
misleading everyone; she felt terribly compromised saying one thing while, indeed, the very
opposite was true.

Acting a role had never been so challenging.
She'd played some awkward parts in the past,
things she hadn't felt well prepared for and
somehow struggled through, but nothing had
ever been like this.

Dancing with Bryn was the hardest, for while
she was sitting next to him at the table at least
she could turn her head to talk to someone else,
distracting herself with pleasant conversation,
but each time he led her back to the dance floor
she felt the pulse of his body against hers and the
blood began to pound heavily through her veins.
Circling the floor with his arms around her, held
close to his hard male body, she had no way of
protecting herself from his magnetic attraction.
She fought it constantly, but each look he gave
her made her heart race, each time his thigh

brushed one of hers she felt the shock waves of reaction rush up her spine, and every time he smiled that devastatingly handsome smile she felt another chink of her armour fall away.

It annoyed her that he was so effortlessly attractive. There wasn't a woman in the room, old or young, who didn't simper up at him in open adoration and the last thing she wanted was to join their number.

'Time to leave,' Bryn said a little later as the ball began to draw to a close. 'I saw that big yawn of yours.'

'It's been a long day,' she said, his fingers curling around hers as he drew her to her feet.

'And it's not over yet.'

'What do you mean, it's not over yet?' she asked with a little frown.

Bryn just smiled as another camera snapped in front of them. Mia forced her fixed lips into a smile as he led her from the room and down the sweeping staircase, waiting until they were in the back of the limousine before repeating her question. 'What do you mean, the night isn't over? I'm tired and I want to go home.'

Bryn leaned forward and closed the sliding

glass panel that separated them from the driver. 'There's something I need to discuss with you. I thought we could go back to my place, where we won't be disturbed.'

She stiffened in her seat. 'I don't want to go anywhere with you. Take me home. *Now.*'

'We'll be in private so you don't need to worry about me having my wicked way with you.'

She gave him a cynical glance. 'You expect me to believe that after the dirty dancing and under-the-table groping routine?'

'You've got great legs,' he said. 'I was just wondering if they felt as good as they looked.'

She rolled her eyes scathingly. 'I can't imagine how you have acquired your Don Juan reputation if that's any indication of the pick-up lines you resort to.'

'It wasn't a pick-up line, it was the truth. You do have a fabulous figure.' He reached for her hand and ran his finger down the length of her bare ring finger. 'Now that we're engaged you need an engagement ring. I have one at my house.'

'How very convenient,' she scoffed. 'I bet you say that to all the girls.'

He ignored her comment and stroked her finger again. 'I want you to wear it.'

She snatched her tingling hand out of his grasp. 'I can just imagine your taste in jewellery—no doubt it's as overbearing and pretentious as you.'

The line of his mouth tightened. 'Actually I think you might be pleasantly surprised.'

'I doubt it.'

'Let's wait and see,' he said and for the rest of the journey remained silent.

Mia sat back in her seat and scowled. She was tired and wanted the safety and security of her own little flat and the familiar, friendly face of Gina, not the company of a man who made her feel as if she was on the edge of a precipitous cliff all the time. No matter how hard she tried to resist his dark good looks she found the pace of her heartbeat increasing every time she met his fathomless blue eyes.

She turned her head away from his silent figure and looked out at the lights fringing the water as Henry drove them along the Cahill Expressway towards the eastern suburbs.

Her sleepy eyes struggled to stay open with the soporific motion of the luxury vehicle. She fought to keep them from closing but in the end she gave up and let her eyelids drift downwards…

Bryn looked down at the silky head resting on his lap, one of her hands on his thigh, her small, neat fingers splayed against him. He watched the in and out of her breathing, the slight movement of her chest lifting the creamy curves of her breasts tantalisingly. Her body was totally relaxed against him; gone was the stiff, defiant little firebrand with her quick-witted tongue, and in her place was a young woman who was breathtakingly beautiful now that the earlier tension had left her body. She had a sweet vulnerability about her, as if she had slipped to his lap in unconscious trust that he would do nothing to harm or exploit her.

He gently tucked a strand of hair off her cheek and secured it behind the small shell of her ear, her soft murmur as he did so making his chest feel a little strange, as if someone had caught him with a tiny fish hook deep inside and given it a quick little tug before just as swiftly releasing him.

He sighed and wondered if he was doing the right thing after all. He was used to women who were happy to play by the rules he set down, took what he offered and were grateful for whatever time and attention he afforded them. Mia Forrester, however, was not likely to appreciate what he had in mind for her and it bothered him. It bothered him a great deal. But he had to find a way to convince her to go along with his plans. Time was running out and this was the only way he could see to solve the dilemma he was in.

Mia woke up as soon as the car came to a halt.

'Hello, sleepyhead.' His glinting eyes met hers, his mouth tilted in a little smile.

She struggled upright, appalled that she had draped herself all over him. She looked outside and saw they were in the driveway of an imposing-looking mansion in the exclusive suburb of Point Piper.

'Is this your house?'

'Yes. Come inside and I'll show you around.'

Mia got out of the car reluctantly. Pretending to be his fiancée in public was one thing; coming back to his house and being alone with him was something else again. She didn't trust him not to insist on another kissing rehearsal. How would she be able to keep a clear head if he decided to take things even further? She was already in over her head as it was. He was exactly the sort of man she'd actively avoided all her dating life. He was too self-assured and too experienced for her to keep at arm's length. She just didn't know how to handle men like him.

Bryn opened the soundproof panel and addressed the driver. 'You can go home now, Henry, I'll see that Miss Forrester gets home.'

'Thank you, Mr Dwyer.' He took off his cap at Mia and added, 'Miss Forrester. Enjoy the rest of your evening.'

'Thank you.'

Mia waited until the driver had left before turning on Bryn. 'I thought I told you I didn't want to come back here with you. I'm tired and I want to go home.'

'You can sleep in tomorrow. It's not as if you have to get up for work.'

'Thanks to you,' she said with an embittered look.

'You can't tell me you enjoyed working in that café, Mia,' he said as he opened the door and ushered her in. 'It was a pittance of a wage and you had to be polite to obnoxious people all day, which I can only assume from what I've seen of you so far was incredibly difficult, if not at times impossible.'

'Not all of them were obnoxious,' she countered with a narrow-eyed glare.

He shrugged himself out of his jacket and tossed it to one side before reaching to loosen his tie. 'Would you like a drink?'

'No.'

He led the way to a sumptuous lounge with stunning views over the harbour. Two luxurious caramel-coloured leather sofas dominated the room, the floor was covered with deep cream carpet and the walls adorned with original paintings from some well-known Australian and international artists. There was a well-appointed bar at one end of the room and an impressive-looking sound and entertainment system along the far wall.

Mia stood looking out at the view rather than meet Bryn's dark eyes. 'How long have you lived here?' she asked.

She heard the chink of a glass behind her. 'A couple of years or so. I wanted a place where the Press can't hound me all the time.'

She turned around to look at him in puzzlement. 'I thought you actively courted the Press. Isn't that the whole reason I'm playing this role for you, to increase your ratings?'

He took a sip of his drink before answering. 'It's one of the reasons you are here.'

She gave him a wary look, her heart beginning to thud unevenly. 'You mean there's more than one?'

He put his glass down and came to stand in front of her. Mia tried to step away but the backs of her legs came up against one of the sofas. She drew in a sharp little breath as she brought her gaze up to his. His eyes were so dark she felt as if she was staring into the moonless midnight sky.

'When you poured that coffee in my lap this morning I thought it would be a good opportunity to give my ratings a boost by pretending to have a whirlwind romance with you, and it worked. The public fell for it, hook line and sinker. Annabelle called me earlier with the ratings for this afternoon's show and they were absolutely phenomenal. The stuff the Press releases tomorrow will ramp them up even more.

But it's not the only reason I have for wanting you to act this role for me a little longer.'

Mia waited for him to go on, wondering what other reason he could have for continuing this ridiculous charade. She wanted it to stop before things got out of hand. She already felt as if she'd stepped over some sort of invisible barrier after he'd kissed her, not once but three times. She wasn't even sure if what she was doing was even acting any more. The more time she spent with him the more the lines blurred between what was real and what was fantasy.

'Jocey mentioned my great-aunt Agnes to you this evening,' he said after a small pause.

'Yes…'

'She's my only living relative and I owe her a great deal.' He let out a small sigh and scored a rough pathway through the dark brown silk of his hair before adding, 'She hasn't got long to live and I would give anything to make her last few weeks of life as happy as they can possibly be.'

Mia was surprised by the sincerity in his voice, he sounded as if he really cared for his great aunt. *Truly* cared.

She found it difficult to fit his public persona

as a thirty-three-year-old filthy rich playboy with
a reputation for shallow, short-lived relationships
with the man in front of her, who obviously cared
very deeply for an ageing relative.

'I'm sorry about your great-aunt's health,' she
said softly. 'It must be an awful time for you both.'

His gaze meshed with hers once more. 'My
great-aunt's only wish is to see me happily settled.
She sacrificed her chance at marriage in order to
raise me when my parents died so suddenly when
I was a child. She gave up everything for me.'

Mia swallowed at the sudden intensity of his
blue-black gaze.

'You see, Mia, a simple engagement might be
enough for the Press and the public, but it is not
going to be enough for Agnes.'

'I-it's not?'

He shook his head gravely. 'No. What she
wants more than anything in the world before she
dies is to see me officially married.'

'M-married?' she gulped. 'Officially?'

'Yes, in front of witnesses, preferably in a
church and legally binding.'

'You surely don't expect me to...' She found
it impossible to finish the sentence in case by

saying it out loud it would somehow make it inescapably true.

'I'm asking you to marry me, Mia,' he said, confirming her worst fears.

She stared at him open-mouthed. Surely she'd misheard him. He couldn't possibly have...

'Of course, I don't expect you to do it for nothing,' he went on evenly. 'I will pay you a lump sum up front and a generous allowance for as long as the marriage continues.'

'You want me to marry you? For real?' She gawped at him incredulously. 'You mean you're actually *serious* about this?'

He frowned at her stupefied expression. 'I'm not asking you to jump off the harbour bridge, Mia, just to wear my ring until such time as it is no longer necessary.'

Mia's stomach felt as if she'd just jumped off Centrepoint Tower, which was a whole lot taller than the harbour bridge. How could she possibly consent to marrying a man she hated? And even worse—for money?

'But marriage?' she asked again, shaking her head in disbelief.

'Yes, as in vows and rings and stuff.'

'Marriage is a whole lot more than vows and rings and stuff,' she said. 'It's a legally binding agreement between two people who are supposed to love one another and promise to do so until death parts them.'

'So we're not exactly up to scratch on all the particulars but we can still pull this off,' he said.

'You sound as if you're discussing some sort of business proposal.'

'That's exactly what I'm discussing. A business proposal.'

Mia frowned as she tried to take it all in. 'You mean this won't really be a real marriage?'

'It will be real in the sense that it will be official and legal. I can't risk someone uncovering it as a sham but as for us being a normal couple...' he hesitated for a fraction of a second before adding, 'well, of course it won't be real.'

She moistened her bone-dry lips. 'So we won't be...you know...'

His dark eyes met hers. 'Having sex?'

'Yes...'

'Not unless you want to.'

Mia felt her cheeks burning but forced herself to hold his gaze. 'Of course I don't want to!'

His expression was contemplative as he held her gaze for several moments before he responded. 'Fine; however, I must insist that for the duration of our marriage you refrain from sleeping with anyone else. I wouldn't want anyone to suspect things are not normal between us if you are seen with someone other than me.'

She gave him a pointed look. 'Do I get to insist on the same rule for you?'

'I will do my best to be discreet if the need should arise.'

'Then I insist on the same for myself. I, too, can be discreet.'

'As you wish, but let me tell you if you put one step wrong I will be extremely angry. I don't want my great-aunt to be upset by any rumours of impropriety.'

'She won't be upset by me,' Mia said confidently. 'At least I don't have any empty-headed bimbos in my background.'

He gave her a droll look. 'As of today I have finished with empty-headed bimbos. You are now, for all intents and purposes, the love of my life, and I expect you to maintain that illusion for as long as is necessary.'

'And I thought my four years at stage school were challenging,' Mia muttered resentfully.

'The challenging part for you will be controlling your propensity for insulting me at every opportunity.'

She gave a cynical snort. 'That's rich coming from the High Priest of Insults. If you weren't such a pompous jerk I wouldn't find it so challenging.'

'If you weren't such an uptight little cat you would see I'm nothing like the public image I project,' he clipped back.

She folded her arms across her chest, her expression full of scorn. 'I suppose you're going to tell me you're really nothing like the Bryn Dwyer the public has come to love and hate. Oh, please. Spare me the violins. Anyone can see you're a self-serving egotist who would stop at nothing to achieve his ends. This crazy scheme of yours to hoodwink your great-aunt is a case in point. What kind of man would openly lie to a little old lady by marrying a woman he has absolutely no feelings for?'

'I happen to love my great-aunt very dearly and I would do anything to make her last days happy, even if it means temporarily tying myself to a shrill little shrew to prove it.'

'Shrill little shrew, am I, now?' She glared at him. 'Well, let me tell you I don't think too much of you either. You're hardly what I'd call the ultimate choice in husband material.'

'You don't have to think much of me,' he said. 'All I want you to do is marry me. We'll sort the feelings end of it out later.'

'I don't have any feelings where you're concerned other than unmitigated dislike.'

'Good. You'd be best to keep it that way. I wouldn't want to complicate things any further with you forming an emotional attachment to me.'

'Where exactly did you go for your ego-enhancement surgery?' she quipped in return. 'Was it horrendously expensive?'

Bryn struggled to hold back his amusement but in the end gave up. His face cracked on a smile. 'I think you are definitely wasted as a serious actor. You have a real future in comedy.'

'Yes, well, this little farce is definitely running along those lines. You're asking me to act a role that is totally immoral. Acting in front of an audience is one thing but acting in front of a dying old lady is another. And marriage! It just doesn't seem right.'

'It will make her happy. That's all I want.'

'I don't want to do this, Bryn; you can't force me.'

He held her gaze for an uncomfortable pause. Mia felt as if she was being slowly but steadily backed into a tight corner. She even wondered if it had been wise to mention the word force. She could see the steely determination in his darker than night eyes and her stomach felt as if something with tiny clawed feet had just scuttled across it.

The sudden silence was like a third presence in the room, brooding and somehow menacing, making the fine hairs on the back of her neck lift one by one.

'I'm hoping it won't have to come to me actually forcing you,' he said. 'At this point in time I'm simply asking you to help me bring a small measure of happiness to an old woman who sacrificed her own to raise me. I am willing to pay you well. I know it will be difficult for you. I also know you hate me, but I can't help feeling you are the one person my great-aunt will take to. She heard us on the radio this afternoon; she already thinks you're perfect for me. There are plenty of women I could ask to play this role, but I know my aunt well enough to know that the only one she will accept as the real thing is you.'

Mia tried not to think of how she was going to explain all of this to her family or friends. Instead she thought about an old lady who had sacrificed her life to raise a child who had been devastated by the loss of his parents. She thought too of the little boy of seven who had suffered such a tragic loss. A little boy with dark brown hair and deep blue eyes, a little boy who had become a man who, as far as she could make out, hid his childhood pain behind a façade of cocksure arrogance.

It wasn't as if it was going to be a real marriage, she did her best to reassure herself. After all, actors did this stuff all the time. God, how many times had Julia Roberts been married on screen? It meant nothing.

It was all an act.

A role to play.

Temporarily.

But still…

'Can I have some time to think about it?' she

asked. 'This is totally surreal. I can't quite get my head around it.'

'Of course,' he said. 'But I'd like you to meet my great-aunt tomorrow; it will perhaps help you to make up your mind.'

She captured her bottom lip for a moment. 'What if I don't agree to marry you?'

His eyes locked down on hers. 'Then you'll be throwing away a fortune.'

Mia gave a tiny swallow. 'Exactly how big a fortune?'

He named a sum that sent a shock wave through her brain. Mia came from a comfortable background and had never really wanted for anything in her life, but the amount of money he was willing to pay was unbelievably generous. The money he'd already given her had helped ease Ellie's situation fractionally but if she could send her thousands it would mean her sister would be out of danger for good.

But marrying Bryn Dwyer?

'If you do decide to take up this offer there will be some legal documents to sign,' he said into the silence, 'a prenuptial agreement and so forth. And, as I mentioned in the car earlier, as my fiancée I'd like you to wear an engagement ring.'

Mia watched as he went across the room to where a large painting was hanging. He shifted it to one side as he activated the code on the concealed safe set in the wall and, opening the safe, took out a blue velvet box before closing it again and repositioning the painting.

He brought the box over to her, took out a solitaire diamond engagement ring and handed it to her.

'It was my mother's,' he informed her.

Mia turned the white-gold ring in her fingers, staring down at the simple perfection of the diamond.

'Try it on,' he said.

She slipped it on her ring finger, not sure whether to be surprised or spooked by the perfect fit. It was nothing like she'd been expecting. There was nothing ostentatious or flashy about it. It was simply a beautiful ring that had once been worn by his mother, a woman who had been torn from his life when he was a small, vulnerable child.

'If you don't like it we can choose something else,' he said into the silence.

'No...no, I like it...it's...beautiful...' Tears welled in her eyes and her throat felt tight, but she wasn't sure why she was feeling so emotional.

'It's not worth a lot of money but it's one of the few things I have left of my mother,' he said, turning away to hunt for his car keys. 'Come on, I'd better take you home. It's nearly three a.m.'

Mia followed him out of the house in silence, the ring on her finger tying her to him in a way no priceless jewel could do.

It's just a stupid old ring, she chided herself, but somehow whenever she looked down at the diamond winking up at her she felt as if something elemental had just taken place in their relationship.

He didn't speak on the journey back to her flat. Mia stole covert glances at him from time to time but his expression was closed. She could see the lines of tiredness around his eyes and wondered what sort of day he had ahead. She knew that working in radio was not just a simple matter of turning up for the time he was on air but that hours of research and preparation had to be put in before and after. She also knew it was a fickle business. A radio personality could be the flavour of the month only to be cast aside the next. Ratings were everything and contracts were cancelled or renewed on what they revealed. But Bryn hardly needed the money. He was a multimillionaire, so whatever satisfaction he got from having his own prime-time show must be motivated by something other than monetary reward. Fame? Prestige? Power? Or was it the desire to be known as something other than who he really was?

'I'll call you later,' Bryn said as he pulled up in front of her flat.

Mia didn't answer. She got out of the car when he opened her door and with her head down began to move towards her front door.

'Mia.'

She stopped as his hand came down on her shoulder and slowly turned around to face him.

'You did a good job tonight,' he said. 'Thank you.'

Her chin lifted in pride. 'So you're finally admitting I can act, then, are you?'

He bent down and pressed a soft kiss to the corner of her mouth. 'That's what I'm paying you to do,' he said as he straightened. 'Goodnight.'

She watched from her window as he drove away, her fingers absently playing with the ring he'd given her, a small worried frown taking up residence on her forehead.

Yes, he was paying her to act, but what if she forgot her script and began to make up her own?

A script that wasn't for the temporary season he had in mind but for much longer?

CHAPTER SIX

'OH, MY God, look at this!' Gina thrust the morning's paper at Mia. 'And this one…and look at this magazine! You're famous!'

Mia looked at the articles spread out before her and forced a stiff smile to her face. 'Hey, I don't look so bad, do I?'

'You look absolutely gorgeous and the Press loved you,' Gina answered. 'Here, listen to this:

The beautiful Mia Forrester, a struggling part-time actor and former café waitress has stolen the heart of Sydney radio personality and multimillionaire Bryn Dwyer, in a whirl-wind romance that has to be seen to be believed. Miss Forrester is a radiant young woman who clearly has taken to her role as Bryn Dwyer's future wife with enthusiasm.

It is rumoured that the wedding will take place within a matter of weeks. The young couple dined and danced the night away at the St Patrick's Children's Charity Ball before spending the night together at Mr Dwyer's Point Piper mansion.'

'I did not spend the night with him!' Mia said indignantly and then, seeing her friend's raised brows, hastily tacked on, 'or at least not the whole night.'

'I know that but it just goes to show you can't believe everything you read in the Press, now, can you?'

Mia lowered her gaze to the photo spread and answered with more than a hint of irony, 'No, you certainly cannot.'

Gina put her chin on her hand and sighed. 'You know, I really envy you, Mia. You're so lucky you haven't had a string of disastrous love affairs in your past like me. That's just so special these days when just about everyone jumps into bed on the first date. Your honeymoon will be so romantic, the memory of your first time together will be something you'll treasure all your married life.'

Mia felt a hot, trickling sensation low down in her belly at the thought of the possibility of Bryn Dwyer becoming her lover.

She hadn't intentionally held back from conducting a sexual relationship with previous boyfriends but neither had she rushed into anything she hadn't felt ready for. She'd always believed making love should be about exactly that—making love, not having sex just for the sake of it. She knew it was perhaps a little old fashioned, but a part of her was proud that she had maintained her standards in spite of peer and popular-culture pressure.

One of her friends had been very ill with a sexually transmitted disease as a teenager and it had made Mia all the more determined to wait until she was absolutely sure it was the right step to take. Besides, she had never been in love with anyone, at least not seriously enough to consider committing herself physically.

Gina gave another dreamy sigh as she flicked through the rest of the articles. 'He's just so gorgeous—look at the way he's smiling at you in this picture. I don't think I've ever seen a man more in love.'

Mia looked over her friend's shoulder and frowned. It was strange, as she was supposed to be the professional actor, but Gina was right; Bryn Dwyer had given a truly brilliant performance as a man totally smitten by love.

'What did your parents think of your news?' Gina asked.

Mia faltered over her reply. 'Um…I haven't actually called them yet…time differences and so on. I'll probably email them later today.'

'What about Ellie? When does she get back from her wilderness trek in the Amazon?'

Mia carefully avoided her flatmate's eyes. She hated lying but Ellie had expressly asked her not to tell anyone. As much as she wanted to break her promise, deep down she understood Ellie's motivations. News had a habit of travelling and if her parents got wind of the danger Ellie was in it could trigger another heart attack for their father. It was going to be bad enough when they got to hear of Mia's impending marriage.

'I'm not sure,' she said evasively. 'She said something about staying on for a little longer. You know Ellie, if there's a crusade she can put her name to, she will.'

'It seems a shame none of your family is here to celebrate your engagement with you.' Gina closed the paper. 'Wouldn't it be absolutely awful if they didn't get back in time for the wedding?'

It would be wonderful, Mia thought privately; that way I won't have to stretch my acting capabilities to the limit. But as she responded verbally she had to yet again draw deeply on her acting experience to sound genuine. 'You know something, Gina, I've always sort of dreamed of a private wedding. The only person I want there is the man I love. If the church was full to the rafters I'm sure I wouldn't even notice a single soul except for the one waiting for me at the altar.'

'You're right.' Gina smiled. 'Who cares who is there as long as your future husband is there, ready and waiting? But I insist on being there—I wouldn't miss it for the world.'

Mia gave her a smile, even though her jaw ached with the effort. 'It will be nice to have you there, Gina; after all, who else is going to catch the bouquet?'

Mia watched from her window as Bryn arrived in front of her flat a short time later in a powerful red Maserati. He unfolded himself from the driver's seat, the casual clothes he was wearing highlighting his height and lean, athletic build as he strode towards her front door. She opened the door at his firm knock and tried not to be over-whelmed by his disturbing presence as he stepped inside.

His eyes ran over her but before she could mumble a single word of greeting Gina came bounding out of her room.

'Wow! I can't believe it's really you.' She stuck out her hand to him. 'I'm Mia's flatmate, Gina. I've been dying to meet you. I absolutely *adore* your show and your column. I'm a huge fan and so are all our friends, but most especially Mia, she never misses your show, right, Mia?'

Mia stretched her lips into a semblance of a smile. 'That's right.'

Bryn smiled as he drew Mia closer, stooping to press a long, searing kiss to her mouth. He lifted his head and looked into her eyes. 'That's what I like to hear—the woman I love is my biggest fan.'

Mia had to wait until they were in the car and on their way before she could vent her spleen.

'Did you have to be so...so completely over-the-top? I'm sure you embarrassed Gina by kissing me like that. It was totally unnecessary. A simple peck would have done.'

He sent her a sideways glance, his eyes glinting darkly. 'I'm not a simple-peck sort of guy. If I'm going to kiss someone I'm going to damn well do it properly.'

Mia felt a fluttery feeling between her thighs at his statement. She was already well aware of his kissing skill and couldn't help wondering what it would be like to experience his whole lovemaking repertoire. She imagined he would be a demanding but consummate lover who would take his partner to the very heights of sensual experience.

Her gaze strayed to his hands where they rested on the steering wheel, her skin tightening all over at the thought of those long, tanned fingers touching her intimately. How would it feel to have him stroke her...?

Bryn caught the tail end of her glance, noting her heightened colour and the agitated look on her face. 'If you're feeling a bit nervous about meeting my great-aunt, don't be. I'm sure you'll take to her immediately; she's that sort of person.'

'I'm not nervous...' she said and began chewing at her bottom lip.

He sent her one more thoughtful look but she had turned her head and was looking out of the window, her fingers playing absently with the engagement ring on her hand.

The private palliative-care unit Agnes Dwyer was residing in had a peaceful atmosphere and was beautifully landscaped with sweet-smelling roses that could be viewed from every window.

Bryn's great-aunt was in a room overlooking a trickling fountain adorned with cupids and dolphins, the sound of wind chimes signalling the movement of the summer breeze across the exquisite garden.

Mia looked at the emaciated figure lying on the bed, the sunken eyes closed, the hollow papery cheeks speaking of a life long lived and now coming to its inevitable end.

Her heart contracted painfully as she glanced up at Bryn. His expression, unguarded for a fraction of a second revealed the depth of his emotions at the loss he must soon face.

'Aunt Aggie,' he said softly, taking his great-aunt's hand in his.

Mia watched as the old woman's eyes opened and gradually focused.

'Oh, darling...you caught me napping.' She struggled upright with Bryn's gentle, solicitous help and met Mia's clear grey gaze at the end of the bed. 'Come here, my dear, and let me look at you. My eyes are not as good as they used to be.'

Mia stepped forward and took the thin hand that had reached for hers. 'Hello.'

'My, oh, my, but you're gorgeous,' Agnes said. 'One of the nurses brought in the papers this morning but you are even more beautiful than the photographs in them.'

'Thank you,' Mia said shyly.

Agnes smiled. 'You are just as I hoped Bryn's future wife would be.'

'I—I am?'

'Yes, indeed. I so wanted him to find someone genuine. You have a big heart; I can see it in those big grey eyes of yours. You are perfect for him.'

Mia felt the daggers of guilt prod at her sharply. She could barely stand to look into the old woman's eyes in case she saw the truth about her relationship with her great-nephew.

'I—I'm glad you think so...' she said, lowering

her gaze and hating herself for yet another lie as she added, 'He's perfect for me too.'

'I knew it would be this way. His parents were the same, you know. When my nephew first met Bryn's mother it was love at first sight.' The old woman gave a sad little sigh. 'But they didn't get the chance to live the life they should have had together…'

Mia could sense Bryn's discomfiture at his great-aunt's disclosure and her heart went out to him again for what he must have suffered. She felt uncomfortable with the way she had judged him so rashly; it didn't seem right to have written him off as a self-serving playboy, given what he'd been through. No wonder he lived life so shallowly when life had let him down so early.

'It was a long time ago,' he inserted gruffly.

'I know, darling, but now that I am facing…well, you know what I'm facing…I can't help feeling that I could have done more for you.'

'That's totally ridiculous and you know it,' he said. 'You've been the most wonderful support. I couldn't have asked for a better guardian.'

'But I wasn't the real thing, was I?' Agnes said. 'I was just a substitute for the real thing. I could never be enough. I could never be your parents, no matter how much I tried to be.'

'Please don't say that…' Bryn said, squeezing her hand gently.

'Darling, darling boy,' Agnes sighed and, giving his hand an affectionate pat, turned her head to Mia. 'You will have to take over from me, sweet child, and love him when I'm gone. It won't be long now…'

Mia swallowed the solid lump of emotion in her throat. She could feel the sting of tears at the backs of her eyes and her chest felt as if someone had clamped it in a vice. Guilt assailed her and passed over her skin like a scalding burn.

'I will love him…for you and for me…' she said softly. 'He's a wonderful man…'

'I'm so very glad you think so,' Agnes said through misty eyes. 'Very few people know the real Bryn, but I can rest in peace now that I know he has found someone who loves him for who he really is. It's not easy being in the public eye, but then you'd know all about that, being an actor yourself.'

'I'm not a very good one, I'm afraid…' Mia said with downcast eyes.

'Your modesty is delightful,' Agnes said. 'But perhaps Bryn was right when he wrote that review, although he was a very naughty boy to put it quite the way he did.' She sent her great-nephew a mock-reproving glance before turning back to Mia. 'You were miscast. You have a de-lightful air of innocence about you which is so rare these days.'

Mia wondered just how innocent Bryn's great-aunt would consider her if she knew what was really going on between her and Bryn.

'We mustn't tire you,' Bryn said to his great-aunt. 'We'll leave you to rest for now. I'll pop by again later.'

'Thank you, darling.' Agnes took Mia's hand again and gave it a tiny squeeze. 'You probably haven't even had time to discuss when you're getting married but personally I'm not a great believer in long engagements. In this day and age, when practically everyone is cohabiting, what is the point? Besides, I haven't got much time left. It would be a dream come true to see my Bryn happily married. I know it's a lot to ask, but I do so want to be there on your special day if it's at all possible.'

'I want you to be there too,' Mia said, swiping at an escaping tear.

Bryn slipped his arm around her waist and drew her closer as he addressed his great-aunt. 'We'll let you know as soon as we have a date set.'

'Thank you, darling...I'm sorry to be such a bother.'

Bryn stooped down to kiss his great-aunt's cheek. 'You could never be a bother. Now, have a good rest and I'll see you later.'

Mia slipped out of Bryn's embrace to kiss his elderly relative, her eyes bright with tears as she straightened. 'It was lovely to meet you.'

'You have made me so very happy,' Agnes said. 'I cannot think of a more wonderful partner for Bryn.'

Mia was blubbering uncontrollably by the time they got back to where Bryn had parked his car. She began to hunt for a tissue when he pressed a clean white handkerchief into her hand, his expression thoughtful as his dark blue eyes met her streaming ones.

'I'm sorry...' she choked out. 'I just can't help it...'

'It's all right,' he said and drew her up against him, his hand going to the back of her head to bring her head to his chest.

'It's just so sad…' she sniffed. 'I don't know how you can bear it…it reminds me of when my granny died…I still feel emotional every time I see someone with grey hair and it's been seven years.'

Bryn kept stroking his fingers through her hair, his chest feeling a little strange as he breathed in the fragrance of her light but unforgettable perfume.

Mia lifted her head to look up at him, her eyes red-rimmed and swollen and her bottom lip still trembling with emotion. 'I feel so guilty lying to her… I know you're going to think this is really weird, or dumb even, but I wish we *had* fallen in love…' She gave another little sniff and added, 'I wish this was really true and not just an act.'

Bryn stared down at her uptilted face and felt another gear shift in his chest. Something warm and indefinable began to slowly spread and then fill him inside as he thought about being loved for real by her.

The only person he had ever felt truly loved by since he'd lost his parents was his great-aunt.

The truth was, he hadn't always been that lovable. Although he'd always denied it, he had been seriously traumatised by his parents' death. He had never been able to find it within himself to forgive the person responsible for taking his parents from him.

He'd been a lonely, angry child and his behaviour throughout his childhood and adolescence had been nothing short of deplorable. Even as an adult he'd been selfish and arrogant, riding rough-shod over people with a ruthless disregard for their feelings. To a very large degree his bad-boy image had propelled him into the success he'd experienced and most of the time he played it to the hilt. The public expected him to be cutting and sarcastic, it was his trademark, but it wasn't who he really was or indeed who he really wanted to be.

'Does this mean you've decided to go ahead with our marriage?' he asked after a little pause.

'I don't see how I can possibly say no,' she answered somewhat grimly. 'Agnes is dying…it seems so unfair not to grant her this last wish, even if it is all an act.' She bit her lip and then released it to add uncertainly, 'I guess I can see it through for a week or two…'

'We have to see this through, Mia, no matter how compromised each of us feels. I don't want her to know this is all an act. It would destroy her.'

'I know…' she said and eased herself out of his embrace. 'I just feel uncomfortable… I'm being paid to be your wife. It just seems so…so…you know…terribly tacky.'

'You're thinking too much,' he said as he unlocked the car. 'It's just money and I have plenty, so you don't need to worry on that score. Think of it as any other acting job. I'm sure every actor has been assigned roles that aren't quite to their taste, but they do it for the money.'

Mia frowned as she got in and fastened her seat belt. It wasn't the money she was really worried about, she knew he had plenty and what he was paying her would hardly make a dent in it, and it would certainly solve her sister's dilemma. It was what he couldn't give her that worried her more. She was being paid to pretend to love a man she had previously thought unlovable, but somehow as he'd held her a few moments ago she had felt a tiny flicker of something deep inside, as if something was trying to make its way out to the surface but was being blocked in some way.

She sneaked a glance at him as he drove out of the car park. His expression was mostly inscrutable except for the tiny glitter of sadness she thought she could see in his dark eyes. But, as if he sensed her looking at him, he reached for his sunglasses on the dashboard and put them on his face and she was shut out once more.

CHAPTER SEVEN

THE next few days passed in a whirlwind of activity that left Mia spinning. There was legal work to be dealt with and, although she felt uncomfortable signing documents that were so legally binding, she did it for the sake of Bryn's great-aunt. She just couldn't stop thinking about the older woman's life coming to an end and how it would impact on Bryn. She was his last living relative. Once she died there would be no one else but him. His final link with his parents would be gone.

As far as she could tell he had spoken to no one about his dying relative. Jocey Myers had only found out by a quirk of fate. There had been nothing mentioned in any of the newspaper articles about Agnes Dwyer's role in his life and certainly no mention of the tragic loss of his parents when he was a child. She wondered if he did it deliberately, as Jocey had suggested, to keep his hard-as-nails image in place or whether there was some other reason.

The Press went wild when the news broke of their impending marriage; requests for interviews flew thick and fast and wherever she went paparazzi followed, hoping for a candid shot of Bryn Dwyer's intended bride.

It made Mia totally rethink her life-long dream to be famous. Now fame was becoming a reality she found she hated it. She couldn't do the most basic things without being followed; even going for her morning run or thrice-weekly visits to the gym became an exercise of subterfuge in order to escape the intrusion of journalists and cameras.

Bryn, on the other hand, seemed to take it all in his stride. He insisted they dine out regularly and she was forced to put on a bright smile and accompany him to yet another high-profile restaurant.

'I don't know how you stand this,' she said at the end of the second week of their engagement. They were in a harbour-side restaurant and had only been seated for three minutes when a rush of fans had come up for autographs and im-promptu phone-camera photos.

'It'll soon pass,' he reassured her. 'Once we're married they'll leave us alone.'

'I certainly hope so…' She toyed with the stem of her glass agitatedly as the *maître d'* ushered the last of the lingering diners back to their tables.

Bryn gave her a quizzical look. 'I thought your goal in life was to be famous. Isn't that what every actor wants?'

She let out a tiny sigh. 'There's fame and there's fame. I guess I didn't really think about it too much…you know… how it would be if I ever made it into the big time.'

'How long have you wanted to be an actor?' he asked.

He watched as her mouth tilted engagingly, his chest feeling that little fish hook tug again. 'I think I was about four or five years old,' she said. 'I'm a middle child and apparently I was always trying to be the centre of attention. It was the Christmas pageant when I was in kinder-garten that finally decided it for me. I was cast as the front end of a donkey in the nativity play and that was it. I decided I wanted to be on stage.

I went to ballet and tap classes and gymnastics and joined the school swimming team and then a junior drama club when I could finally persuade my parents to pay for it. My poor mum was run off her feet ferrying me back and forth to everything.'

'Tell me about your family.'

'Well...' She smiled fondly as she met his eyes. 'My mum and dad have been happily married for nearly thirty years. They are wonderful, just as parents should be. I have a sister, Ashleigh, a year older than me, who's married to Jake and they have a son and a little daughter. I adore them. I have a younger sister, Ellie, who's adopted. She's fantastic.'

'So you're a close family?'

Mia gave him a very direct look. 'There's nothing I wouldn't do for my family. I would give my life up for any one of them at a moment's notice.'

He returned her look for a lengthy period before asking, 'Have you told them about us?'

She chewed her lip for a moment and lowered her gaze. 'My younger sister is...somewhere in the wilds of the Amazon. My parents are overseas at the moment with Jake and Ashleigh and the kids, so I haven't got around to it. I'm not sure I want them to rush home for a wedding that's not really real. Apart from a quick visit to London a few years ago, this is the first European trip my parents have had since they were married, so I didn't want to ruin it for them.'

'I hardly think attending their daughter's wedding is going to ruin their holiday,' Bryn said.

Mia looked up at him with a slight frown. 'But it's not as if it's a proper wedding. What would be the point? Besides, as soon as your great-aunt...' she faltered over the words '...passes away the marriage will be annulled.'

He gave her another lengthy look, his eyes very dark as they held hers. 'What if my great-aunt doesn't die in the next few weeks?'

Her hands gripped the edges of the seat. 'Wh-what do you mean?'

'I was speaking to her oncologist earlier today,' he said. 'Her condition has improved remarkably since she heard the news of our engagement. Her spirits have lifted and she's making a real effort to eat again; the last bout of chemotherapy hit her hard but she's put on a bit of weight and has more energy.'

'But that's a good thing, surely?' Then at his wry look she stumbled on, 'I mean...for your great-aunt, that is... maybe it's not so good for me...us...well, you know what I mean...'

'Of course it's a good thing for Agnes, but it may mean we will have to continue our charade for a bit longer than I initially expected.'

Mia lowered her gaze to her wine glass as she considered the possibility of being married to him for months on end. The very last thing she wanted was to hurry up his great-aunt's death, but living with a man as his wife for several months was just asking for trouble, especially with a man like Bryn. She was already fighting an attraction to him that was threatening to get out of hand.

'How...how long do you think we'll have to stay married?' she asked after a little silence.

He picked up his wine glass and took a sip before answering. 'It's hard to put a time on it. Three or four months.'

She swallowed thickly. 'That's a long time...'

His mouth twisted. 'It's not such a long time when you're the one who is terminally ill.'

'No...no, I guess not...'

He reached into his top pocket and handed her a card with the name of one of Sydney's top bridal designers on it. 'I've organised an open account for you to purchase what you need. I've also deposited funds in your bank account which you will no doubt need to draw on in preparation for our wedding.'

Mia found it a little unsettling for him to be discussing their marriage in such terms. She couldn't help wondering what it would have been like planning a proper wedding, with both parties excited at celebrating the most important day of their lives. Her sister Ashleigh's wedding to Jake after four long years of separation had been one of the most moving experiences she'd ever had. There hadn't been a dry eye in the house and even now, more than a year later, the photos of that special day still brought tears to Mia's eyes.

How different would her wedding day be? She'd be marrying a man who was using her as a career hoist, not to mention colluding with him in fooling his dying great-aunt that her greatest wish for him had come true.

But then, she reminded herself, she had her

own reasons for going through with it. Her sister, for one thing, but then there were those feelings that kept her awake at night. Feelings she really had no business feeling...

'After the wedding we will be going on a short honeymoon,' he announced into the silence.

'A honeymoon?' She stared at him, her heart thudding in alarm. 'Whatever for?'

'All newly married couples go on a honeymoon.'

'I know, but surely in our case it's not necessary. I mean, what would be the point?'

'It will be a good opportunity for us to get to know one another a little better out of the way of the Press,' he said, and then added with a teasing grin, 'You never know, you might even start to like me a bit.'

She gave him a castigating look without answering.

'There is something else we need to discuss about our living arrangements,' he said after another tiny but telling pause.

Her gaze flicked nervously back to his dark and unwavering one. 'I get to have my own room, right?' she asked.

'If you want one.'

She blinked at him. 'What do you mean, if I want one? Of course I want one!'

'There is the perplexing little matter of my housekeeper,' he said. 'She comes in three times a week.'

'So…what are you saying?'

'If Marita sees two beds being used instead of one she'll immediately suspect something is up and it will be all over the papers the next morning.'

'Can't you pay her to keep quiet or something?' she asked hopefully.

He shook his head. 'There are very few people I would trust even under payment.'

'I don't suppose you could dismiss your housekeeper…I mean, I can cook and clean if you want me to.'

'I have no intention of dismissing my housekeeper. She has a young family to support.'

'So what are you suggesting? That we play musical beds or something on the days your housekeeper is there?'

'I don't know. I haven't thought it through.' He gave her a sexy grin and added, 'Who knows, you might have decided to sleep with me by the time we are married.'

She looked at him incredulously. 'You surely don't think I'd take things *that* far?'

'I will leave that decision entirely up to you. The agreement we made is that this will be a paper marriage but if you at any time wish to change your mind about consummating it, I will be perfectly happy to do so.'

'Just because we will be sharing a house temporarily doesn't mean we will be sharing anything else, housekeeper or no housekeeper,' she said with force.

He gave a casual shrug and reached for his wine. 'There are plenty of women in your position who would jump at the chance to share my bed and my body.'

'And I'm quite sure legions of them have, but you can forget about putting my name in your little black book. I'm not interested.'

'I promise to keep my hands to myself as long as you promise the same.'

She sent him a frosty look. 'You seem very confident I'll be tempted by you.'

He smiled wickedly. 'You have been so far. Every time we've kissed you've got all hot and bothered.'

'I was acting!'

His smile tilted even further. 'Maybe, but when you kissed Clete Schussler on stage that night it didn't look half as convincing as when you've kissed me.'

Mia wasn't sure how to defend herself. Clete Schussler was undoubtedly a damn good kisser but, acting or not, he was not quite in the same league as Bryn Dwyer. Was any man?

'It was first-night nerves,' she said. 'I'd only ever been the understudy. We had six weeks of rehearsal but I hadn't kissed him before.'

'I'd only met you a few hours before I kissed you for the first time, and as far as I'm concerned we did a much better job.'

Mia was inclined to agree with him but didn't want to give his already oversized ego another boost. She gave him a stony look instead and remained silent.

Bryn smiled at her brooding expression. 'Come now, Mia. Admit it. You might not like me all that much but you are very definitely attracted to me.'

She rolled her eyes disdainfully. 'You'd have to try a whole lot harder to get me to agree to a physical relationship with you. No one's managed it so far and...' She stopped when she realised what she'd inadvertently revealed.

He frowned at her in puzzlement. 'No one's managed what so far?'

'Um...' Her cheeks flared with heat and she had to look away from his probing gaze.

Bryn leaned forward a fraction, his expression becoming incredulous as realisation dawned. 'You mean you've never actually had sex?'

She didn't answer.

'You're what...twenty-four years old and you've *never*—?'

'Will you keep your voice down?' she hissed back at him. 'Someone will hear you.'

He sat back in his chair and shook his head in amazement. 'I can't believe it.' He gave a quick self-deprecating laugh. 'I employ a virgin to act as my wife. Hell, I must be out of my mind.'

She gave him a resentful scowl. 'I don't know why you're making such a big deal about it. Anyway, most men still maintain the double standard by having sex indiscriminately until they decide they want to choose a wife and future mother of their children, then they want someone who hasn't been around the block too many times.'

'No wonder you couldn't act that role,' he said. 'I was right after all. You didn't have a clue how to play a seductress.'

'I do know what goes on, you know,' she said. 'I'm not totally clueless.'

His midnight-blue gaze twinkled. 'So you've gone south solo a few times to see how things work?'

Hot colour flooded her face but she forced herself to hold his taunting look. 'That's none of your business.'

He gave a soft laugh at her discomfiture. 'Don't be embarrassed. I think it's delightful. It shows you're not a total prude.'

'There's nothing prudish about being selective with whom you share your body, especially these days. You don't know what you might catch.'

'No, indeed there isn't, but you surely can't have had a lack of opportunity. You're a beautiful looking young woman with a great body. You must have been fighting men off for years.'

Mia berated herself for reacting to his compliments but she just couldn't help feeling a glow of warmth as his words washed over her. She disguised her reaction by saying airily, 'I've had a few boyfriends.'

'But no one has ever tempted you to sleep with them?'

She met his eyes once more. 'No one so far.'

He gave her an unreadable little smile as he signalled to the waiter for the bill. 'Then I guess the road is wide open to me.'

She hitched her chin up a fraction as he drew her to her feet. 'Better men than you have tried and failed,' she informed him coldly.

His eyes were alight with challenge. 'No, what you mean is, better men than me have tried and given up. I don't believe in giving up. If I want something, I make damned sure I get it.'

'Not this time,' she said with overblown confidence. 'If you don't keep to your side of the deal I won't be obliged to keep to mine.' She drew in a breath and tacked on recklessly, 'I will go to the Press with the truth about our relationship. Then what will your great-aunt think of you? She'll know you lied to her when she was most vulnerable, and no matter what your motive was, I don't think she will forgive you.'

His eyes started to smoulder as they held hers. 'If you do that I will be forced to play dirty with you, Mia. Don't make me show you how ruthless I can be.'

She didn't get a chance to respond, for he grasped her hand and practically dragged her out of the restaurant and over to his car.

'Get in,' he bit out as he opened the passenger door.

She got in but only because people were starting to look at them, and she didn't want to create a scene. She sat stiffly in her seat and watched as he strode around to the driver's side, his expression dark with simmering anger.

He waited until they were on their way before he spoke, his voice chillingly hard and determined. 'I swear to God, Mia, if my great-aunt's last weeks or months of life are ruined by you leaking something to the Press you will seriously regret it. I'll make sure of it. I'll throw everything at you. You will never work again—in any industry. Don't think I wouldn't or couldn't do it, for I can, and I will.'

Mia felt deeply ashamed of her impulsive threat but there was no way her pride would allow her to show it. 'I'm not scared of you,' she tossed back. 'You can threaten me all you like but I'm not scared.'

'Then perhaps you should be,' he said. 'Didn't you read the fine print on those documents I sent for you to sign?'

She felt an icy shiver pass over her skin. She had read the documents but only briefly. The legal terms had been offputting enough, but when Gina had come home unexpectedly and started to peer over her shoulder Mia had hastily signed the highlighted sections and stuffed the documents back in the return express envelope and posted it.

'Let me refresh your memory,' he continued when she didn't respond. 'There is a clause on page five that states that if you, the undersigned, at any point during the duration of our marriage reveal intimate information about our relationship to the Press or anyone else, you will have to repay all monies already allocated to you as well as the legal fees in the subsequent defamation case I will immediately activate with my legal advisors.' He sent her a quick, brittle glance and continued in the same chilling tone, 'In case the legalese is a bit hard for you to understand, let me put it in layperson's terms: I am going to take you to the cleaners.'

Mia compressed her lips as she thought about how much money might be involved. It was a daunting scenario and one she was going to have to do her very best to avoid. Her parents were comfortably well off but certainly not in Bryn's league and, while her brother-in-law, Jake, was extremely wealthy, she didn't want to involve him in a public fight that could turn out to be very nasty. And until Ellie was out of danger she had no choice but to play by the rules.

Bryn's fierce loyalty to his only living relative was certainly admirable and perhaps a clue to whom he really was as a person, but she didn't like the thought of being on the receiving end of his wrath if things didn't go according to plan.

'Anyone could have heard you in there,' he said into the tight silence. 'You know the deal. In public we are like any other normal couple in love, if you want to pick a fight with me then please have the sense to do so while we are in private.'

'I won't go to the Press if you stick to your side of the deal. You can pay me to be your wife but there's no amount of money on this earth that I would accept to become your lover,' she said stiffly.

'Fine.' He shoved the car into top gear. 'But as I said, if you ever change your mind just let me know.'

She gave a scornful snort. 'As if.'

His eyes clashed with hers for a brief moment. It was hardly more than a fraction of a second but Mia had to turn away.

She felt herself being thrust back in her seat as he floored the throttle—the atmosphere crackled with tension and her stomach gave a funny little quiver when he drawled, 'We'll see.'

CHAPTER EIGHT

Two days before the wedding Mia visited Agnes at the palliative-care unit. She had deliberated over it for days, wondering if it was wise to see the old lady without Bryn present, but the temptation to find out more about his background from the person who knew him best was far too tempting to resist. She didn't tell Bryn about her intention to visit his great-aunt the night before when they'd had dinner together in yet another of Sydney's premier restaurants. For days after their terse exchange when she'd threatened to go to the Press he had been distant and formal with her in private, although whenever they were in public he acted the role of attentive fiancé with his usual and somewhat unnerving expertise. For all his charming smiles and spine-tingling touches when others were looking, Mia knew he was still angry with her, and she also knew, if she was truly honest with herself, she really couldn't blame him. He wanted his great-aunt's last weeks of life to be as happy as possible, and she had threatened to jeopardise his plans, with what would appear to him a callous disregard on her part for what his great-aunt would feel on hearing such a revelation.

The nurse on duty led the way to Agnes Dwyer's room and, after announcing to the old lady she had a visitor, she gave Mia a quick smile and closed the door on her exit.

'Mia, my dear, what a wonderful surprise! How lovely to see you,' she greeted her with a warm smile. 'I thought you'd be far too busy organising your wedding to take time out to visit me.'

Mia came towards the bed and held out the bright red, orange and pink gerberas she'd brought with her. 'These are for you…I thought you might like something colourful for your room.'

'They're gorgeous, my dear. What a lovely gesture. Most people give me dull, old-lady-type flowers. I'm fed up with lavender and lily of the valley. These are marvellously cheery. I'll get the nurse to put them in water. Now, come and tell me how the wedding plans are going.' She patted the bed beside her. 'Sit next to me here...go on, I won't bite.'

Mia perched on the edge of the bed and the old woman reached for her hand. 'I was hoping you'd come to visit me,' she said. 'Bryn comes in twice a day but I wanted to speak to you privately.'

'Y-you did?'

'Yes,' Agnes said. 'I thought it would be nice for us to have a little woman-to-woman chat.'

'Oh...'

A small silence fell into the room. Mia could hear the rattle of a tea trolley further down the corridor, and further away the sound of a relaxation CD playing in another patient's room.

Agnes finally spoke. 'Bryn won't be an easy man to live with, Mia. I feel I should warn you, since it's really my fault you're rushing into marriage so quickly. You haven't had time to get to know him properly. I know you love him, that's more than obvious, and he very clearly is devoted to you, but you might find things tough going once the first rush of love passes.'

Mia remained silent, her heart doing a funny hit-and-miss beat in her chest.

'I always knew it would take a very special woman to melt the ice around Bryn's heart,' the old woman said. 'He's been so guarded for so long. He has never let his emotions rule his heart before. I'm so very glad he found you.'

'Thank you...' Mia said softly, her eyes falling away from the unwavering gaze of Bryn's only relative.

'You see, Mia, Bryn has never really come to terms with his parents' death...'

'It was an accident, wasn't it?' Mia inserted into the silence.

'Yes, but it wasn't really anyone's fault,' the old woman said. 'The young driver of the car that hit my nephew and his wife head on lost control on a bend. He'd only had his licence a short time. He wasn't speeding and the inquest found that no alcohol or drugs were involved. It was just one of those accidents that wouldn't have even happened if Bryn's parents had driven past just a few seconds later.' She shook her head sadly. 'It's hard to imagine how different things would have been just for the sake of a few seconds...'

Mia swallowed the lump of emotion clogging her throat. 'You've given up so much for Bryn...'

'Yes, that's true, but he needed me and I was happy to step into his parents' role. He was such an unhappy little boy. What Bryn needed was his parents, but due to circumstances beyond our control he could never have them. He has harboured such ill feeling towards that poor man for most of his life. Forgiveness is something he finds very hard. I guess you could call him stubborn.' She gave Mia a little smile. 'No doubt you'll come up against his strong will from time to time.'

'I'm sure I'll be able to handle it,' Mia said. 'I'm pretty strong-willed myself.'

'You will need to be, my dear. Bryn can be a wonderful friend but a powerful and deadly enemy. But I am sure with your gentle love you will be able to help him let go of the past and find it in himself to forgive.'

'I'll do my best,' Mia promised.

Agnes gave her hand a little squeeze. 'Are you excited about the wedding?'

'Um…nervous really…'

'That's understandable. It's been such a rush.' She gave a little sigh. 'I wish I had more time allotted me, then you would have had more time to prepare for your life together. It doesn't seem fair for you to be fast-tracked into marriage without the time to plan things properly.'

'It's fine…really,' Mia reassured her. 'It's what Bryn and I both want.'

'You know, Mia, I was in love once,' Agnes said softly. 'It happened late in life; I was so excited. We were going to be married but when Bryn's parents were tragically killed my fiancé wasn't keen on having an instant family. He gave me a choice. It was either him or Bryn.'

'And you chose Bryn…'

'Yes. But then I had to act as if I was no longer in love with my fiancé. It took some doing, I can assure you, especially when after a few months he married someone else and had a child with her. I was heartbroken but I had to carry on.'

Mia felt the sting of tears at the backs of her eyes for what both Bryn and his great-aunt had been through. How had she coped with losing the man she loved? And how had Bryn as a child so small and defenceless coped with such a terrible loss without it leaving permanent scars?

'Bryn shut down emotionally after his parents died,' Agnes went on sadly. 'I tried to ease him out of it but I'm afraid he resisted all my attempts to get him to talk about it. It was as if his parents had been permanently erased from his mind. He never mentioned them. He still doesn't. Even the photos I kept about the place would disappear without explanation. I gave up in the end.'

'He speaks so fondly of you…'

'Yes, he's a darling, but as I said you'll have your work cut out for you. I never thought he'd ever settle down. No one did. It's a miracle it happened while I was still alive to see it.'

Mia moistened her lips self-consciously. 'Yes…it is…'

'I can't tell you how much it means to me to see him so happy at last,' the old woman went on. 'I am so excited about the wedding. I am living for the day.'

Mia gave a tight swallow. 'So am—' Her words faded as a tall figure suddenly appeared in the doorway.

'Is this a private meeting or can anyone join in?' Bryn asked as he entered the room.

'Bryn, darling, you're early,' Agnes greeted him warmly. 'Look at the lovely flowers Mia brought me.'

Mia watched as he stooped to press a kiss to his great-aunt's cheek, trying to work out if he had overheard any of their conversation. She could imagine he would be very annoyed to find her discussing his past with his only living relative. How long had he been standing there?

'And how is my gorgeous fiancée?' He turned and pulled her into his embrace, lowering his head to place a scorching kiss on her lips.

She forced herself to meet his glinting dark gaze once he'd lifted his mouth from hers. 'Hi...'

He held her look for what seemed a very long time before he turned back to his great-aunt. 'Are you all set for the wedding?'

'Yes, dear,' Agnes responded. 'The nurse is coming with me, as you arranged. I can hardly wait.'

Bryn took Mia's hand and tucked it through his arm, looking down at her with an inscrutable expression on his face. 'Nor can I, isn't that right, sweetheart?'

'Um...that's right...' Mia gave a shaky smile.

Bryn waited until they were outside in the car park before he spoke, his tone and frown accusatory. 'Why didn't you tell me you were coming to visit my great-aunt?'

'It was a last-minute decision,' she said, lowering her gaze. 'I thought she might like some flowers.'

'What did you talk about?'

'Not much…the wedding arrangements and stuff…'

His frown increased at her evasive answer. 'You weren't tempted to act on your threat to spill the beans?'

'No, of course not.' She looked up at him. 'I didn't even mean it when I said it, much less intend to ever act on it. I was angry at you. I would never do anything to upset her.'

His eyes were hard as they clashed with hers. 'You'd better be telling me the truth.'

'I am telling you the truth but if you don't stop glaring at me like that your great-aunt along with the staff around here might draw their own conclusions about the true state of our relationship,' she warned him.

He let out his breath in a ragged stream, his mouth tilting wryly. 'You're right. I must have pre-wedding nerves or something.'

'It's not too late to call it off,' she said, fiddling with her car keys in an effort to avoid his eyes again. 'I'm sure Agnes would understand if you told her the truth.'

'No.' His tone was implacable. 'Our marriage is going ahead come hell or high water. It's what she wants more than anything. Besides, Annabelle rang me just before I arrived here and told me my latest ratings. My popularity is at an all-time high. If we pulled the plug now it would destroy my credibility and totally ruin my career.'

She gave him a haughty look as she unlocked her car. 'I hope you're not expecting empathy from me if that should ever happen.'

'It's not going to happen, Mia,' he said with steely determination. 'Because we are going to be husband and wife in forty-eight hours, and like I just said to Agnes: I can hardly wait.'

'You look absolutely beautiful,' Gina gushed as Mia put the final touches to her bridal make-up two days later. 'I can't wait to see Bryn's face when he sees you.'

Mia gave herself a critical look in the mirror.

The skirt of the white satin and tulle gown was voluminous and emphasised her slim waist, and the close-fitting strapless top showcased her upper body to maximum effect. Her make-up was subtle but highlighted her clear grey eyes and the creamy texture of her skin. Gina had done her hair for her, setting it in Velcro rollers first before arranging it on top of her head in a sophisticated style that made her feel like a princess.

'I guess I look OK,' she admitted grudgingly.

'More than OK,' Gina said, then added with a tiny sigh, 'But it's a pity your family aren't here to see you.'

Mia pretended to be concentrating on attaching her veil rather than meet her friend's eyes. It had been the hardest thing she'd had to do so far when she'd called her parents the previous night and told them she was getting married the following day. In many ways it had been the performance of her life. She had managed to convince her entire family that it was the real deal, including Ellie, who had called her from Brazil saying she was going to be released in forty-eight hours thanks to Mia's efforts on her behalf.

Mia had told each of them of her whirlwind love affair with Bryn and how very happy she was. Her parents had initially been disappointed that she had left it so late to tell them but when she explained her reasons they understood her concern that they have the holiday they had planned for so long without interruption.

Ashleigh, so much in love with her own husband, was an easy person to convince. She had fallen in love with Jake Marriott at first sight, so there was no way she would have ever questioned Mia's story.

'I think that's Henry now,' Gina said, peering out of the window.

Mia took a steadying breath as she reached for the bouquet of white roses, her stomach turning over in trepidation.

There was no way out now.

She was going to be married to Bryn Dwyer within the hour.

Officially.

Legally.

Temporarily.

'Ready?' Gina asked with a huge excited grin.

Mia smiled until it hurt. 'I'm ready.'

* * *

Bryn turned to watch Mia walk up the aisle; she had refused his offer of someone to give her away in the absence of her father and decided to do it all by herself with just her flatmate as bridesmaid.

He caught the eye of his great-aunt, who was sitting with a nurse in attendance. The sheer joy on her frail, pale face was all he had ever hoped for and it made him a little less guilt-stricken about how he'd engineered his relationship with Mia.

From the very first moment his eyes had clashed with Mia's in that café, he had wanted her. And when she'd come to the station and bawled him out he had wanted her even more. He liked her fighting spirit. He liked the way she stood up to him defiantly when every other woman would have given in. He also liked her soft heart; the way she had openly cried when she met his great-aunt for the first time had touched him very deeply. And though he knew it was probably terribly chauvinistic of him, he couldn't help but feel pleased she hadn't slept around. It seemed likely she would be less inclined to be indiscreet with someone else, but on the other hand it meant he would have his work cut out for him convincing her to sleep with him, which he very much wanted her to do. He had thought of nothing else; his desire for her throbbed constantly in his blood, until he could barely think about anything else. He saw her as a particular challenge, and the one thing he liked in life was a stiff challenge. She hated him and he looked forward to the challenge of making her fall for him just like every other woman had in the past. It had nothing to do with his feelings. He had no intention of complicating his life with emotions that could only come to grief. He liked her, of course; who wouldn't? She was feisty and quick-witted and when she wasn't tearing strips off him her personality was sweet and caring.

He looked down as Mia came and stood next to him, the scent of her flowery perfume filling his nostrils, her tentative smile as she met his gaze through the film of her veil making his throat feel unusually tight. He cleared it discreetly and faced the front, straightening his shoulders and taking a breath as the priest began the ceremony in a solemn, authoritative tone.

'Dearly beloved, we are gathered here...'

CHAPTER NINE

MIA stood very still as Bryn turned to lift her veil from her face at the priest's command to kiss the bride. His dark gaze meshed with hers for an infinitesimal pause before he lowered his mouth to hers. A soft sigh escaped from her lips and disappeared into the warmth of his mouth as it covered hers in a lingering, passionate kiss that sent rivers of sensation through her body.

You're not acting, a little voice inside her head began to taunt her but she refused to acknowledge it. Of course she was acting! That was what Bryn was paying her to do, to convince the world that she was in love with him when the very opposite was true.

She hated him.

No, you don't. That same little voice was back and even more insistent this time.

'I do.'

Mia hadn't realised she had spoken the words out loud until she saw the quizzical look on Bryn's face as he straightened from kissing her.

'We've already said that bit,' he whispered with a teasing little smile.

'I—I know…I was just…' She gave up in relief when the priest announced the signing of the register would take place before the bride and groom would exit the cathedral.

Once the register was signed and some photos taken, they made their way back down the aisle to the strains of Handel's music, the congregation and interested bystanders swelling towards them as they stepped out into the warm summer sunshine.

The reception was held at the same hotel as the ball had been, the room beautifully and lavishly decorated, and the champagne flowing freely by the time they arrived from having the official photographs taken.

Speeches and toasts were made, the cake was cut and the bridal waltz performed, cameras still flashing madly until it was finally time for Bryn and Mia to leave.

Gina had a tussle over the bouquet with several other young women but she was victorious in the end, although the bouquet she held proudly aloft was suspiciously short of a few blooms.

The ever-present journalists pressed forward as Bryn helped Mia into his car, their microphones outstretched. 'Where's the honeymoon going to be, Mr Dwyer?' one of them asked.

'How long will you be away?' another pushed in.

'No comment,' Bryn said and closed Mia's door. He waved to everyone before he got in the driver's seat and leaning across gave Mia a long, sensual kiss for the benefit of the cameras.

Mia was already feeling a bit light-headed from all the champagne she'd consumed and his kiss made her head spin even more. She sank against him, her senses reeling at the erotic message being communicated by his lips and tongue.

He lifted his head and, smiling once more for the Press, he gunned the engine and they were away, balloons and tin cans and streamers trailing in their wake, the shaving-foam message 'Just Married' scrawled all over the back window.

'How are you holding up?' Bryn asked the silent figure beside him a few minutes later.

She sent him a rueful sideways glance. 'My face aches from smiling all the time.'

He gave a soft chuckle of laughter. 'Yeah, so does mine.' He glanced in the rear-view mirror at the bouncing cans and pulled over to the side of the road to remove them, placing them in a rubbish bin on the pavement before getting back in behind the wheel and easing the car into the traffic.

Mia stared down at the two rings on her left hand. It hardly seemed real that she was sitting next to a man she hadn't even met in person a little over a month ago. And now she was going on a honeymoon with him to his private retreat in the Queensland Sunshine Coast town of Noosa.

'Do you think the Press will follow us?' she asked to fill the little silence.

'I shouldn't think so,' he answered. 'I think now the wedding has come and gone their interest will die down. It has to. All they were really interested in was whether or not we were really getting married. No one thought I would ever do it.'

Mia gave her rings another twirl, not trusting herself to chance a glance his way. 'Your great-aunt seemed to be very happy for you.'

'Yes, she was.' His eyes flicked to her briefly. 'I guess I should thank you for playing the role so well. You must have acted the beautiful-bride part before. You were a natural.'

'I've been to a lot of weddings,' she said and then added in a self-deprecating tone, 'besides, the priest tells you what to say. It's hardly challenging. It's like having an Autocue to prompt you.'

He smiled as he took the turn to the domestic terminal. 'I guess the challenging bit is yet to come.'

Mia decided not to respond. She'd been steadily panicking about the bit to come all day and wondered how in the world she was going to negotiate her way through it.

Ever since she'd spoken with his great-aunt Mia had felt increasingly confused about her feelings towards him. She could still taste his kiss on her lips and it worried her that once they were alone she wouldn't have the resolve to keep her growing attraction to him under control. He was hard enough to resist while she hated him. How much more tempting would he be if she started to like him?

But you do like him, the little voice in her head

returned. She tried to block it but it kept on filling her head with nonsense.

You're in love with him.

You want to spend the rest of your life with him.

You want to have his children.

She clutched at her bag with both hands, staring down at the rings on her finger that bound her to him.

It couldn't possibly be true. How could she love a man who had destroyed her career with a few words he'd written, thinking nothing of it, as if it were a simple game of sport?

She was just falling under his sensual spell like every other silly woman who didn't have a measure of self-control. She would just have to try harder to avoid becoming yet another of his conquests.

Falling in love with Bryn Dwyer was too dangerous.

Their relationship was temporary.

She had to remember that.

'Come on, Mia.' Bryn's voice broke through her reverie as he opened her door a few minutes later. 'Our plane leaves in forty minutes. We need to check in before the flight closes.'

* * *

The flight to Maroochydore took an hour and a half and Mia was glad that for most of it she had slept. She woke just as they were coming in to land, the lights of the coastal town situated on the south bank of the Maroochy River twinkling in the clear night air.

Bryn had organised a hire car for them and as soon as the luggage was collected he began the thirty-minute drive north to Noosa.

'Have you been to Noosa before?' he asked once they were on their way.

'Yes, but it was quite a while ago, ten years at least. We came on a family holiday,' she answered. 'It might have completely changed by now.'

'That's what so nice about it up here,' he said. 'It never really changes. Sure, there've been developments up and down the river and along the coast, but nothing like the massive high-rises on the Gold Coast. Noosa National Park is a great place to walk through. You can even do a beach crawl if you want. There are quiet, shady bays or great surf spots, so whatever your mood you can usually find somewhere to relax.'

'I remember the national park. My sister Ashleigh hated the long walks my parents kept taking us on. Ellie wanted to stop and look at every bit of wildlife and I kept running on ahead, driving my parents crazy in case I got lost, which I seem to recall I did on more than one occasion.'

'You must have been a cute kid,' he said after a little pause. 'I envy your family life. It must have been wonderful having such a loving environment to grow up in.'

'It wasn't always fun and games,' she said. 'I love my sisters but we fought a lot when we were younger. I guess all kids do.'

There was another lengthy silence.

'I often wondered what it would have been like to have a brother or a sister.'

She looked at him. 'It must have been very hard growing up without your parents.'

'It was. But I learned to cope. My great-aunt did the best she could but I wasn't the easiest person to be around at times.'

'Do you have any photos of your parents?'

'I guess I have them somewhere.'

'Why don't you have them out on show?'

'I'm not the sentimental type,' he said. 'It's in the past and I'm only interested in the future.'

Mia decided to step out on a limb. 'Your

great-aunt said you used to hide any photos of your parents when she put them out. Why did you do that?'

He gave her a hard little glance. 'You sound as if the two of you had a very cosy chat.'

'I just wanted to find out a bit more about the man I was marrying.'

'And did she enlighten you?'

Mia frowned at his sharpened tone. 'There's no need to be so defensive.'

'I'm not being defensive. I just don't appreciate you interfering in things that don't concern you.'

'I think I have the right to know what has made you the way you are.'

'Why? So you can reform me, to make me more user-friendly?'

'You're way beyond reform,' she snapped back irritably. 'I wouldn't even bother trying.'

'Good. Then at least we know where we both stand.'

Mia frowned as she sat back in her seat with a sigh of frustration. He was like a closed book. As soon as she tried to prise open the pages he would just as quickly snap them shut. She knew he was hurting—she could almost feel it coming off him whenever the subject of his childhood was raised. It was like an aura surrounding him. He didn't trust life not to hit him from the left field again when he was least expecting it.

He reminded her of Ashleigh's gorgeous husband, Jake. He had hidden his inner pain behind a façade of cynicism that had very nearly destroyed her sister's life and his own as well. But Ashleigh's enduring love had found a healing pathway to his soul.

Did she have what it took to do the same for Bryn? And more to the point—did she even want to try?

'I think you'll like my house,' Bryn said after another lengthy silence. 'I had it designed specially.'

As olive branches went it wasn't quite what she had been hoping for but she realised he was making an effort and she forced herself to accept it in the spirit in which it was given.

'I'm looking forward to seeing it,' she said.

Mia looked around her a few minutes later in awe. She had been expecting Bryn's beach hideaway to be luxurious but nothing had quite prepared her for the sheer brilliance of the design that gave him sweeping views over the Noosa River on one side and the beaches and national park on the other. The house was on three levels and was tucked in the bush land that fringed the area, offering a level of privacy that was unbelievable. There were no curtains at any of the main windows—they weren't necessary as the house was set higher than the rest of its neighbours and the thick surrounding bush was an effective screen.

'What do you think?' Bryn asked as soon as he'd shown her the entry level where the main lounge was situated as well as the kitchen and spacious dining area.

'It's…wonderful…' She turned to look at him. 'No wonder you love coming here. It's like a private paradise.'

'Come and I'll show you the rest of the house from the top floor down,' he said, leading the way to the open-plan stairs.

Mia followed him as he showed her the three large bedrooms on the top level. A wall of built-in wardrobes gave each room a feeling of space, as did the minimalist décor and pristine white bed linen on the beds. Each *en suite* had a large, free-standing bowl-like white basin on top of a simple vanity and a big walk-in shower, and the floor and walls were tiled with marble the colour of flecked sand.

He led her back down the stairs to the lower level, where an impressive gym was set up in a large room that led out through French doors to a lap pool in the private garden in which frangipani trees scented the balmy night air.

'Wow...' Mia breathed in wonder as she looked around. 'You sure know the way to an exercise junkie's heart.'

Bryn chuckled as she bent down to trail her fingers in the water of the pool to test its temperature. 'I was wondering how you maintained that stunning figure of yours. Now I know.'

Mia felt his compliment wash over her like the warm silk of the water around her fingers. She straightened from the pool and tried to hide her reaction but he caught one of her hands and brought her to a standstill right in front of him.

He stroked the backs of the knuckles of one hand over the heightened colour of her cheek in a movement so gentle her breath came to a stumbling halt right in the middle of her chest. Her stomach gave a little flutter, just like the wings of a trapped moth inside a tiny confined space.

She moistened her suddenly dry mouth at the dark intensity in his midnight-blue gaze as it locked with hers.

The perfumed air swirled around them, wrapping them in a sensual mantle of summer warmth, the exotic atmosphere tipping the balance of distance Mia had desperately tried to maintain between them ever since their marriage was formalised that afternoon.

She felt sure he was going to kiss her. She could feel it along the exposed skin of her arms and legs, the tiny hairs on the back of her neck lifting in anticipation as his head came inexorably closer. Her eyelids fluttered closed as his mouth touched down on hers with breath-like softness, as if the moth from inside her stomach had somehow escaped and landed ever so gently on her lips.

Bryn lifted his head a mere fraction, his mouth still so close she could feel the movement of air from his breath over her acutely sensitive skin.

Two beats of silence passed before he lowered

his mouth back to hers, the pressure increasing subtly and tantalisingly. Mia felt the full rush of her blood surging through her veins at the first stroke of his tongue over her lips. She parted her lips and he entered her mouth with gentle but firm insistence, searching for her tongue and mating with it possessively.

Mia felt the prickling of her breasts as he drew her closer into his embrace, her nipples tightening, while her legs and spine felt as if they had been instantly liquefied when one of his hard thighs slipped between hers. She leaned into his hold, her body craving more of his touch, her senses on fire where his hardness probed her softness. Desire exploded inside her, running like a hot stream that threatened to get out of control now it was finally unleashed. She tried to pull it back, tried to get her responses under some semblance of control, but it was impossible. His mouth was like a lighted taper to the spilled fuel of her need, sending hot, licking flames to every single part of her body. She could feel the fullness of her breasts aching for his touch and almost unconsciously began to press herself closer. His erection burned and pulsed against her and she heard his low groan of spiralling need as he deepened the kiss even further.

Without taking his mouth off hers he pressed her back against the wall of the house, one of his hands going to her breast, cupping it through the thin fabric of her top, his thumb rolling over the hardened point of her nipple. Mia felt her breath trip over something invisible as he lifted his head from her mouth, his dark eyes glittering as they held hers for a tiny pause.

Her stomach gave a complete somersault as he slid his hand beneath her top, the warm glide of his fingers over her bare flesh sending her senses into a tailspin. He pushed aside her lacy bra and brought his mouth down to her breast, his lips closing over her nipple and suckling gently until she felt as if he had pulled on an invisible string that was attached to her feminine core. She felt each delicious tug on her sensitised flesh, the tiny arrows of delight like spot fires being lit throughout her quivering body.

His lips left her breast to return to her mouth, this time with increasing urgency, as if he was not quite in control of his reaction to her. She felt his struggle to hold back, the increasing tension in his body where it pressed so temptingly against hers and the latent strength in his arms as he hauled her even closer.

Her hands were in the dark brown silk of his hair, her mouth kissing him back with all the passion of her nature. Her tongue flirted with his, danced with his and became boldly intimate with his, while her heart raced with breakneck speed and her body pulsed with escalating need.

She heard him give another low, deep groan as he wrenched his mouth away, looking down at her with eyes ablaze with unalleviated desire.

It was a moment or two before he spoke but when he did he did so with an ironic twist to his mouth. 'I can only assume from your unbridled reaction to me just now that none of your previous would-be lovers had a comprehensive gym and pool with which to impress you.'

She injected her tone with disdain. 'So you can kiss. Big deal. So can most primates, even chimpanzees and gorillas.'

He gave a soft chuckle that tugged on that invisible string again. 'That's not all I can do, baby. If you continue to respond to me like that—

virgin or not—I'm not sure this is going to stay a paper marriage for very long.'

'You shouldn't have kissed me in the first place,' Mia said. 'It's not exactly as if we have an audience right now.'

'I know, it was a bit unfair but you were so tempting I couldn't resist one little kiss. You have such a beautiful mouth when it's not slinging insults my way.'

'I wouldn't sling insults your way if you would just keep your hands and mouth to yourself.'

'I seem to remember your hands and mouth doing their own little bit of wandering.'

'You're imagining it. I was trying to get away.'

He gave her another taunting smile. 'That was some struggle you were putting up.'

She gave him a withering look without answering.

'In case you're wondering, there is no housekeeper we have to act in front of here,' he said. 'The place is maintained by the neighbours. I pay them a fee to keep an eye on things when I'm away, but while we are here we will have absolute privacy.'

He held the French doors open for her and

once they were indoors added, 'You can have whichever bedroom you like.'

'Which one is yours?'

'Are you asking because you want to avoid it or to share it?'

She gave him a glittering glare. 'What do you think?'

He held her defiant look for a little longer than was comfortable. Mia felt herself inwardly squirming under his steady surveillance and wondered if he could see the truth written on her face even though she did her level best to disguise it.

She wanted him.

For the first time in her life she had come face to face with a man who was temptation personified. Her flesh was still tingling from his touch and she knew if he took even one step towards her and took her in his arms again she would not have the strength of will to resist him.

'Go to bed, Mia,' he said after a short, throbbing silence. 'Otherwise I might be tempted to ravish you right here and now.'

'You wouldn't dare.'

His night-sky eyes grew even darker and his

voice when he spoke was gravel-rough. 'Don't play with matches, sweetheart. I'm sorely tempted to finish what we started out by the pool and one look from you is all it will take to get the flames going again.'

Mia turned for the stairs, forcing herself to go at a dignified pace even though she felt like bolting.

'Goodnight, little virgin wife of mine,' Bryn said, his tone distinctly mocking.

She gritted her teeth and with one last blistering look over her shoulder, opened the first bedroom she came to and closed the door on his taunting smiling face.

CHAPTER TEN

MIA headed straight for the *en suite*. Shutting the door, she stared at her wild appearance in the mirror, her hands clutching the edge of the vanity to steady her trembling legs.

She had to learn to control herself around him! What was she thinking, kissing him back like that? It was totally crazy. It was just asking for the sort of heartbreak she could well do without.

She turned around and, leaning back against the vanity, released a heavy sigh. Of course, resisting him would be a whole lot easier if he weren't so damned tempting. Those dark blue eyes positively smouldered with sensuality every time they locked with hers. And those lips! What woman could resist a kiss that felt as soft as a butterfly landing on an exotic bloom, or not respond when the same kiss turned into something deeply erotic with the determined thrust of his searching tongue?

She looked down at her breasts and suppressed a little shiver of reaction as she thought of his mouth around her nipple. He had been so very close to tipping her over the edge if only he knew it.

She gave a little scowl as she reached for the shower tap.

Maybe he did know it.

The shower was just what she needed; it was cool and refreshing and washed away the dust and damp stickiness of long-distance travel.

It had been a long day and tiredness was creeping up on her, making her sway on her feet as she wrapped the soft, fluffy white towel—bigger than any towel she'd ever seen before—around herself like a sarong.

The bed beckoned her as soon as she left the *en suite*, its wide white-feather softness looking like a cloud of comfort in the middle of the floor.

She gave the room a quick, sweeping glance for her suitcase so she could retrieve her nightwear. She'd seen Bryn carry their luggage upstairs earlier but there was no sign of it in here.

She gave a little shrug of tired indifference and slipped the towel off, climbing in between the cool sheets and laying her head down on the soft-as-air feather pillow as she closed her eyes with a sigh of relief...

'So guess who's been sleeping in my bed?'

Mia's eyes sprang open at the deep, lazy drawl, the bright glare from the overhead light making her wince as she struggled upright, clutching the sheet to cover her nakedness.

'*Your* bed?' she gasped, her heart thudding in alarm as she registered that he was wearing nothing but a towel slung loosely around his waist.

Bryn gave her an indolent smile. 'And here I was, thinking it was going to take me the best part of the week to convince you to sleep with me.' He reached for the edge of his towel and dropped it to the floor.

Mia's eyes nearly popped out of her head. She suddenly realised she was staring and quickly flung the sheet over her head. 'For God's sake, cover yourself!' she croaked.

He gave a deep chuckle of laughter. 'Haven't you seen a naked man before?'

'Yes,' she said, her voice muffled from under the sheet.

'So what's the problem?'

'My nephew is five years old, that's what's the problem.'

'So he's got a bit of growing to do, but we all end up more or less the same.'

Mia wasn't so sure about that. She'd seen plenty of toned male bodies at her local gym, admittedly covered by close-fitting gym gear, but Bryn's was something else again—especially naked.

She felt a little tug on the sheet covering her and clutched at it in panic. 'What are you doing?' she shrieked when it slipped out of her desperate grasp.

Bryn's gaze burned as it ran over her and she hastily crossed her legs and covered her breasts with her hands. Her words of protest locked somewhere in her throat as he stepped towards her, her mouth going dry and her heart threatening to make its way out of her chest when he sat down next to her, his muscled, hair-roughened thigh touching her smooth one.

'You're in my bed, which I can only assume means you've changed your mind and now want to sleep with me,' he said.

'I—I didn't know it was your bed.'

He stroked a finger over the upper curves of her breasts where her hands couldn't quite conceal them. 'Don't be shy, Mia. I want to look at you. All of you.'

Mia could hardly breathe; his touch was so light but so very tempting. She could feel the stirrings of desire deep within her and there was nothing she could do to control them. Electricity fizzed along her flesh wherever he touched; even the air seemed to be charged with it. She could feel the crackling tension as his eyes roved her slim form, lingering on the length of her tightly crossed legs and what she was desperately trying to hide from him.

'Uncross your legs, Mia,' he commanded gently.

She shook her head, her lips tightly compressed, not trusting herself to speak.

'I want you, Mia, and I know you want me,' he said. 'I can see it in your eyes, I can feel it in your kisses and I can even smell it on your skin.'

She wished she could deny it but she could smell it herself. The delicate feminine fragrance of desire, the silky liquid that betrayed her vulnerability to him as nothing else could do. He had only to touch her where she most ached to be touched and he would feel it for himself. She could almost feel the thick, smooth glide of his finger moving inside her, stretching her in preparation for his possession.

'It's just hormones,' she said, somewhat breathlessly. 'You shouldn't be feeling flattered at all.'

She could tell he didn't believe her by the laughing glint in his eyes but he didn't press the issue. Instead, he patted her thigh and stood up, not even bothering to hide his erection.

'I'll leave you in peace. I was just teasing. I know you'll come to me when you're ready.'

'You'll be waiting a very long time,' she said with much less conviction than she'd intended.

'I can be patient,' he said, holding her defiant gaze. 'Besides, there are some things in life that are well worth the wait. It makes the prize all the more valuable if you've had to wait for it, don't you think?'

She gave him a sour look. 'If you want a prize, go and enter a meat-tray raffle. I'm not on offer.'

He picked up his towel and wrapped it around his waist once more, a smile still playing around his mouth. 'Sweet dreams, Mia. I'll be in the next room if you want me.'

'I don't want you,' she said but she knew it was more for her own benefit than his.

He picked up the sheet off the floor and spread it over her, tucking her in like a child, stooping to place a soft kiss to her forehead. 'So you keep saying but we both know it isn't true.'

'I suppose someone with the ego the size of yours could only be expected to say something like that,' she bit out resentfully. 'Has there ever been a woman you haven't been able to lure into your bed?'

'Not so far.'

'Poor misguided fools,' she muttered. 'I wonder if there's a support group for them all. It should be called BDCO.'

'What does that stand for?'

'Bryn Dywer's Cast-Offs,' she said. 'Life-time membership free in exchange for a broken heart.'

His shoulders shook as he laughed. 'As far as I know I haven't broken any hearts irreparably,' he said as he reached for the door knob. 'Sleep tight. I'll see you in the morning.'

Mia let out a slow, prickly breath as the door

closed behind him. If she wasn't very careful hers could well be the first heart he would damage beyond repair. If she was honest with herself, she was more than halfway to being in love with him as it was; it wouldn't take too many more of those scorching kisses of his to make her go beyond the point of no return.

Mia woke to brilliant sunshine and the chorus of birds, the distant roll of the ocean in the distance filling her with instant energy. She tossed the sheet aside and came up short when she saw her suitcase next to the built-in wardrobe. Bryn must have brought it in during the night or the early hours of the morning.

A feathery sensation passed over her at the thought of him seeing her sleeping in that big bed, perhaps uncovered and totally vulnerable. She'd been hot during the night and recalled throwing the sheet off at one point until the cooler air of the morning had made her reach for it again.

She gave herself a mental shake and quickly unpacked a bikini and a two-piece sports outfit and trainers from her case and dressed quickly, tying her hair in a high pony-tail.

The house was quiet as she came downstairs but she saw signs of Bryn having had a cup of tea in the kitchen. The kettle was still warm and his cup was rinsed and placed upside down on the draining board.

She heard the clang of weights below her in the gym downstairs and pictured him working out, no doubt lifting three times her body weight as if it were nothing. She decided against joining him. She'd seen enough of his body last night and didn't need reminding of how fabulously toned and muscled he was.

Besides, it was a beautiful day and she could hear the ocean calling. Hard exercise was what she needed to clear her mind from the disturbing images that kept creeping in. Images of her pinned intimately by Bryn's hard body, his hips moving in time with hers as they both climbed towards the summit of sensual release. She could imagine he would be an exciting and demanding lover; every time he'd touched her she'd felt the hot charge of sexual energy pass from his body to hers.

She let out a frustrated breath and set a brisk pace as she ran down the steps leading to the footpath to the beach.

* * *

There were a few surfers already out riding the point break on Main Beach and she jogged along until she came to the pathway leading to Noosa National Park. She followed the coastal track looking out over Laguna Bay and then on to Boiling Pot and Dolphin Point, the growing heat of the morning making her turn just past Winch Cove to head into the cooler shadows of the melaleuca and tea-tree forest.

The honey-sweet smell of the white-canopied bush filled her nostrils as she jogged past gnarled banksias and spiky pandanus. Bush turkeys scratched around the undergrowth and overhead she heard the flap of large wings and looked up to see a pair of glossy black cockatoos flying past.

Further along the track she passed a young couple who were walking hand in hand, their easy-going, loving chatter striking a note of regret in Mia's chest.

How wonderful it would be to be loved like that, she thought. She wanted to be loved the way her sister Ashleigh was loved by her husband, Jake, the way her parents had loved each other for nearly thirty years.

But what she wanted was impossible; Bryn

wasn't the thirty-year-relationship type. Thirty days was too long for him. He wasn't interested in continuing their association past the point of his great-aunt's death. And that could be a matter of just a few short months or possibly even weeks.

The track veered back to Laguna Bay and Mia ran on down to Main Beach, and, leaving her shoes and outer gear on the sand, headed for the waves in her red and white bikini.

She swam the length of the beach, which ran parallel to the popular shopping and restaurant strip of Hastings Street. She turned at the rocky outcrop at one end to go back the way she'd come, the water warm but still refreshing. Every so often a swelling wave would pick her up and let her down again in a gentle rolling movement before it gathered force on its way to the shore.

The sun burned down with intense summer heat and when she waded back through the wash to the sand she could see the numbers on the beach had swelled. Young children were playing at the water's edge with buckets and spades, their parents close by, where several colourful umbrellas were already up in defence against the scorching rays of the sun.

She sat and looked out to sea, hoping for a

moment to gather her thoughts before returning to Bryn's house. But even after sitting there soaking up the warmth of the sun for several minutes she had to finally acknowledge that her vigorous run and swim hadn't been able to do what she'd hoped they would do. It was impossible to avoid any longer the truth that was as persistent as the waves as they drummed against the shore.

She couldn't escape it any more; there was no running away from it even if she ran around the world and back twice over.

She was in love with Bryn Dwyer.

She wasn't sure how it had happened. She had thought him the most detestable man alive and yet somehow over the past few weeks he had become the very focus of her life. She couldn't imagine how her life was going to be without him in it once their marriage was brought to its inevitable end. How would she cope with hearing him on the radio every weekday or reading his acerbic comments in his weekly column? Perhaps once his great-aunt was no longer around he would even joke about his publicity stunt, making a fool of Mia in front of the whole of Sydney, telling his listeners he'd married a twenty-four-year-old virgin who couldn't act to save herself.

'I thought I might find you down here.' Bryn's deep voice suddenly sounded above her.

Mia looked up at him in surprise. 'I...I went for a run...'

His eyes swept over her reddened features. 'So I see.'

She turned back to the sea. The sight of him in nothing but a pair of board shorts and trainers was far too unsettling. 'I've just had a swim and now I think I'll have a little sun-bake for a while.'

'Have you had breakfast?'

'No.'

'Aren't you hungry?'

'No,' she lied.

'Have you had something to drink?'

'No...'

He stretched out the large beach towel he'd brought with him next to where she was sitting. 'Here, lie down on that and I'll go and get you some water.'

Mia turned onto her stomach so she could watch him as he walked back along the promenade to a café on Hastings Street. She saw several female heads turning as he went past, his tanned and muscular but lean frame obviously as attractive to others as it was to her. She gave a little sigh and rested her chin on her hands and closed her eyes.

He came back in a few minutes with a bottle of water and some fresh fruit salad and handed them both to her.

She met his eyes briefly. 'Thank you.'

He sat down on the edge of the towel and looked out to sea. 'How did you sleep?'

'Fine,' she said between mouthfuls of juicy mango and tangy pineapple. 'I like listening to the sound of the ocean. It puts me to sleep every time.'

Bryn wished he could say the same for himself. He'd spent a great deal of the night tossing and turning restlessly, his body still on fire. When he'd taken her bag into her room once she was asleep it had been all he could do not to join her in the bed and pull her into his arms. His desire for her was beyond anything he'd ever experienced before. It gnawed at him relentlessly, making his body ache to possess her. He could feel it now just sitting next to her on the sand, her trim, golden body so close he could smell the hint of vanilla on her skin in spite of the exercise she'd taken.

He turned to look at her and asked, 'What would you like to do today?'

'I don't know...sun-bake and stuff... What did you have in mind?'

'If I told you what I had in mind you might slap my face.'

Mia stared at the piece of kiwi fruit she'd just speared with her plastic fork, her skin prickling all over as she felt the weight of his studied gaze. 'Don't you ever think of anything else besides satisfying your bodily urges?'

He leaned on one elbow, his long, tanned legs stretched out beside hers, his expression teasing. 'Is that why you're an obsessive exerciser? To control your own bodily urges?'

She gave him a chilly little glance. 'I happen to believe in living healthily. The human heart is a muscle like any other. Daily exercise is essential to keep it in good working order.'

'There are other ways of exercising the heart,' he pointed out. 'I could show you if you like.'

'No, thank you.'

He laughed and, picking up a handful of fine sand, began to trickle it over her up-bent thigh.

'Stop that!' She slapped his hand away and began dusting off the grains from between her legs.

'Come in and rinse it off with me,' he suggested, springing to his feet and holding out a hand.

Mia scowled at him but her hand slipped into his regardless. He pulled her to her feet and, releasing her hand, issued her an irresistible challenge. 'I'll race you to the water.'

'You're on,' she said and took off at full speed for the ocean. She had to skirt around a toddler and his mother at the water's edge, which cost her valuable seconds, but she made it to the first breaker and would have beaten him convincingly except he grabbed one of her ankles and tugged her backwards.

She came up spluttering and in revenge scooped a handful of water up and tossed it at his face. 'You cheated!'

He ducked her liquid missile and caught both of her hands in his, pulling her towards him. 'I warned you once before, sweetheart, I don't always play by the rules.'

A gentle wave at her back pushed her even

closer to him and he steadied her with his hands on her waist, his eyes, even bluer than the water around them, locking on hers. She moistened her mouth as his head came down, her eyes closing on her soft sigh as his lips found hers. It was a deeply sensual kiss, made all the more alluring because they were skin on skin in the warm water. Mia had never felt so aware of her body before. She could feel the tightening of her breasts and the melting of her bones as he deepened the kiss. The waves rocked against them, leaving her in no doubt of Bryn's thickening erection pressed so tantalisingly against the naked flesh of her lower belly. She writhed against him, wanting more of his burning heat but lower, where a hollow ache pulsed for him to fill.

After a few breathless minutes Bryn lifted his mouth from hers and looked down at her with a mocking glint in his eyes. 'I can only assume that your rather convincing performance was for the benefit of the crowd on the beach.'

Mia was temporarily lost for words. She hadn't given the crowd a single thought. All she had thought about was how he made her feel and how much she wanted him.

'That's what you're paying me to do, isn't it?' she said at last, her tone sounding terse and embittered as she pulled herself from his hold and stalked back through the waist-deep water to the sand.

Bryn turned to watch her make her way through the foamy wash and frowned. 'Yes…' he said but the words were lost on the waves as they rushed to follow her to the shore. 'Yes, it is.'

CHAPTER ELEVEN

MIA gathered up her things and waited on the promenade for Bryn, who had stopped to help a small child who had tumbled over close to the water's edge. She watched as he crouched down and gently set the toddler back on his feet, handing him his tiny plastic bucket and spade, his warm smile doing something all mushy and wobbly to Mia's insides.

The child's mother rushed up to thank him and after exchanging a few words he picked up his sports shoes off the sand and walked over to where Mia was waiting.

'Your boy-scout deed done for the day?' she queried with an arched brow.

He frowned at her tone. 'I happen to like kids. Is there a law against it?'

'I thought playboys avoided them like the plague.'

He sent her an inscrutable sideways glance as he bent to tie his trainers. 'But I'm not a playboy now, am I? I'm a married man.'

'Only temporarily,' she reminded him, 'and only on paper,'

'That paper is already starting to burn at the edges,' he said as he straightened to look at her. 'Could be it's a pile of ashes by morning.'

Mia didn't answer but she felt a sensation of something hot and liquid flood her lower body at his arrogantly confident statement. She had never met a more sexually compelling man in her entire life and she knew it would take every single gram of her will-power to resist him.

She swung away and began to walk at a brisk pace but within two strides he was alongside her, his beach towel rolled up under one arm.

'Do you fancy a walk through the park or have you had enough exercise for the day?' he asked as they came to the Noosa Heads Surf Life-Saving Club building.

Mia would have loved a cool shower but the thought of going back to the house with him where they would be on their own was a lot more disturbing than a walk through the national park, where at least there would be others about.

'I'd love to,' she said. 'I cut my run short. I only ran as far as Winch Cove as I was getting so hot. I came back through the bush.'

'We can walk to Alexandria Bay for a swim if you like. There are usually less people there, as it's a bit further along the circuit.'

'That sounds good.'

'Wait here while I get us some water to carry,' he said as they came to a shop.

Mia waited as he purchased some bottled water and they were soon on their way, walking in silence under the shade of the eucalypts that fringed the walkway to the national park.

They were not far from Boiling Pot when Bryn took her arm to stall her. 'Look,' he said, pointing above their heads.

She looked up and saw a mother koala perched in the fork of a eucalypt, a tiny baby clutching at her back.

'Oh, wow!' she said excitedly. 'Aren't they adorable?'

Bryn smiled at her. 'This is a natural habitat for them. I occasionally see them in my garden but they generally avoid suburbia if there are dogs about.'

'It's so wonderful to see them out in the wild instead of behind bars at the zoo,' she said as they continued walking along the path.

'Zoos have their place,' he said. 'Think about all the breeding programmes that have been set up specifically to protect endangered species.'

'I know but it seems so sad that animals can't run free as they are meant to do. My sister Ellie is a bit of an animal-rights campaigner. She's told me horror stories of what some people do to animals for financial gain. I had no idea people could be so cruel. I wonder if their conscience ever bothers them at night.'

'It takes all types, I guess,' he agreed, suppressing an inward frown.

They walked on a bit further until they came to Dolphin Point. Mia joined some other tourists who were peering over the cliff to see if there were any dolphins about, but as far as she could tell there was no sign of any in amongst the rolling waves.

'Have you seen any there before?' she asked Bryn as they continued on.

'Sometimes—that's why it's called Dolphin Point. There are several whale-watching tours you can take on the Sunshine Coast, and you often can see dolphins on them as well as humpback whales.'

'I went on one of those the last time I came here,' she said with a wry grimace. 'I was seasick the whole time. I had to be taken to hospital to be rehydrated. Ellie was totally disgusted with me for spoiling the trip.'

'Well, I guess I'd better strike that off the entertainment list for this week.'

'Oh, I'm much better now,' she said. 'I've been out sailing with friends lots of times and haven't had any trouble.'

'You sound like you have a very busy social life.'

She sent him a reproachful little glance from beneath her brows. 'Yes, well, I used to.'

'Just because we are married doesn't mean you can't have friends.'

'But no male friends, right?'

He stopped walking, snagging her arm before she could go on without him. He turned her around to face him, his fingers sliding down to the slender bones of her wrist. 'Male friends are fine if they remain platonic, although I still find it hard to believe any man could look at you without thinking how it would feel to make love to you.'

Mia felt her skin lift as his dark eyes ran over her, all her senses going on full alert at the feel of his long fingers around her wrist, where she was sure he could feel her pulses already leaping.

'Not all men have an insatiable appetite for sex,' she said. 'And the ones I associate with would never dream of tainting our friendship with repeated attempts to get me into bed.'

He gave a little grunt of cynicism. 'That's only because they're probably gay or already involved with someone else. Anyone else would have to be dead from the waist down not to notice you and want to have you as soon as they could.'

Mia felt as if the hot summer air was alive with bristling tension as she held his gaze. His desire for her was like a living, breathing entity. She could feel it burning through her skin where his fingers encircled her wrist, and she knew if it hadn't been for the sound of other hikers coming towards them on the track he would have pulled her into his arms and kissed her senseless. And what was more—she wouldn't have stopped him.

He released her wrist and stepped aside to make room for the tourists, the frustration at being interrupted evident to her in the way his jaw was set, even though he offered the group a polite greeting in response to theirs.

He waited until the group was well ahead before he resumed walking, asking after a few more strides, 'Were you disappointed none of your family could make it to the wedding?'

Mia quickly averted her gaze to look at Granite Bay, a small, rocky beach below them. 'No, why should I be? It wasn't as if it were real. Who knows, our marriage could even be over before they get back? I could probably have got away with not telling them at all.'

He gave her another sideways glance, a small frown settling between his brows. 'When did you tell them?'

She met his eyes briefly before turning to concentrate on stepping over the tree roots on the sandy pathway. 'The day before the ceremony.'

'Hardly enough time for them to get back,' he observed. 'Why did you leave it until then?'

'I hated lying to them. I wasn't sure I'd be able to pull it off in front of them on the day. A last-minute telephone conversation was much easier to handle. I figured there was no way they could get back in time and see the truth for themselves. I can act in front of strangers, even some friends, but my family is another thing entirely.'

Bryn frowned as she walked ahead, her back stiff as she strode out to put as much distance as she could between them. His fairly limited experience of family life had made him insensitive to what she might have felt lying to her family and friends about their relationship. He'd assumed the money he was offering her would settle any of her misgivings, but it was clear she was having a hard time of it now.

His conscience gave him another sharp nudge. He had sought a quick-fix solution to his own problems without truly considering the impact on her. Yes, he'd achieved his goal of fulfilling his great-aunt's dream for him, also securing her considerable estate, but what about Mia's hopes and dreams? He'd crushed them with a few ill-chosen words, got her removed from the company, dropped by her agent and practically blackmailed her into a temporary marriage with him.

A marriage she couldn't wait to get out of.

He drew in a breath that felt like pain at the thought of their marriage ending soon. He'd become used to having her around to spar with him. He'd also become a little too used to having her soft mouth beneath his. But the terms he'd laid down were temporary. As soon as his great-aunt passed away Mia would be free to move on.

But what if their marriage was no longer temporary? What if their relationship was no longer just an act, but real and vibrant and passionately fulfilling for both of them?

She said she hated him but he knew in spite of it she was attracted to him. What would it take to get her to agree to a more permanent relationship with him?

He lengthened his stride and caught up with her. 'Do you remember when I said no one thought I'd ever go through with marriage?'

She turned to look at him. 'Yes...'

'The truth is, Mia, if you hadn't come along when you did I probably would never have married.'

Mia wasn't sure where this was leading. 'You have something against marriage?' she asked.

'Not entirely,' he said. 'I recognise that it occasionally works, but close to fifty per cent of marriages end in divorce, often acrimoniously. I wasn't sure I wanted to add to the stats.'

Her forehead creased in a frown as she pointed out, 'But you're going to add to them anyway now that you've married me temporarily.'

His dark gaze was trained on hers. 'If we divorce we don't have to do it acrimoniously.'

'*If?*' She gave him a startled look. 'What do you mean, if?'

'When you think about it there's at least a fifty per cent chance of things working out between us,' he said.

'One has to really admire your optimism but I'm afraid in this case it's totally inappropriate.'

'What? You don't think we could make a go of it? Arranged marriages are conducted all over the world where the couple neither like nor know each other initially and yet many of them go on to live very happy lives together.'

'Arranged marriages are an insult to women!' she said, beginning to stomp along the path once more. 'It's utterly barbaric to be forced into a marriage with a perfect stranger or someone decades older than you.'

'Marriages have been arranged for centuries,' he countered as he worked hard to keep pace. 'In fact, the notion of a couple falling in love and marrying is a very recent one. Before about two hundred years ago couples married for political reasons or for the sake of securing family property and asset-building or to strengthen community relationships. Of course, affection often occurred in ages past but it wasn't a given.'

'I always knew you were living in the Dark Ages. Where exactly did you get your doctorate in chauvinism?'

He smiled at her sarcasm. 'I'm just quoting history, Mia. Our marriage has just as much chance of being successful as any other; in fact, it may even have more chance.'

'I can't imagine how you came to that conclusion,' she said as she pushed a broken melaleuca branch out of her way. 'I dislike you intensely and I can't see that changing unless you undergo some sort of immediate character reconstruction.'

'As I said previously—you might think differently after a few days alone with me.'

'If the last twenty-four hours is any indication

I'm afraid you're in for a big disappointment if you're expecting me to subscribe to your fan club.'

'Look, Mia, I'm just asking you to try and get to know me as you would any other person. You're so prejudiced against me you can't see me for who I am.'

'Here we go again.' She rolled her eyes expressively as she turned back to face him, her hands on her hips. 'The re-play of the I'm-nothing-like-my-public-persona speech. Give me a break.'

'Damn it, Mia,' his voice rose in frustration, 'why won't you just give us a chance?' His dark eyes held hers. 'Will you at least consider the possibility of our marriage becoming a little more permanent?'

'Define what you mean by a little more permanent. Are you talking months or years?'

'I'm talking about you sleeping with me.'

It was a moment or two before she could get her voice into gear. 'I see.'

'I want you, Mia. You know that. I've wanted you from the moment I met you.'

The silence of the bush surrounded them, closing in on them until Mia felt as she was being cut off from the rest of civilisation.

She was alone with him, alone with him and her unruly, traitorous desire for him, which was getting harder by the second to control.

'You only want me because I'm the first woman to have said no to you.'

'That's not true,' he said. 'It's much more than that.'

'You're surely not going to tell me you've suddenly discovered you're in love with me,' she said with a brittle look. 'That would be about as low as anyone could go.'

He took a moment to answer, his expression giving little away. 'I have some feelings for you, yes.'

'No doubt lust is at the top of the list.'

'It's up there, yes, but so too are admiration and respect. That's more than I've felt for anyone else in the past.'

'Wow, I feel really honoured,' she said mockingly. 'I bet you say that to all the girls when you set out to seduce them.'

'I'm not trying to seduce you for the heck of it, Mia,' he said. 'I really want a relationship with you.'

'A *temporary* relationship,' she put in. 'Where

you get to wave the chequered flag when it's all over—when you get bored or find someone else a little more interesting.'

He didn't answer immediately and it made Mia wonder if he did in fact care something for her. She unconsciously held her breath as his eyes shifted away from hers to stare out to sea. He turned back to her after a moment and handed her one of the bottles of water he was carrying. 'I can't promise you forever, no one can.'

'What exactly are you offering?'

'A relationship for as long as it works for us.'

'So at the first rocky patch we encounter you'll be off to find your next candidate.'

'All I'm asking is for you to think about it, Mia. We're in this marriage for the time being and it makes sense to put in some kind of effort to see if it could work out between us.'

'I can't see how two people who hate each other can make a go of marriage, especially considering the way ours came about.'

'You don't really hate me. I admit you've done a great job of acting like you do but I see the way you look at me when you think I'm not watching. You're seriously attracted to me.'

Her eyes shifted away from his. 'You're imagining it.'

'Am I?'

'Of course.'

'Little liar,' he said, capturing her chin to force her to meet his eyes. 'You want me just as much as I want you. I can see it in those big grey eyes of yours.'

Mia could feel her heart begin to thud when he pulled her closer, his arms coming around her to hold her to his hard frame. His bare chest was hot and slick against hers as his mouth came down on hers, searing her with a kiss full of erotic promise. His tongue was hot and hard as it thrust through the shield of her lips, curling around hers and urging it into a sensual dance that was totally irresistible. A deep ache of longing pulsed low in her belly, the feel of his aroused length pressed up against her increasing her desire to a point where she completely forgot they were standing in the middle of a bush track where anyone could see them.

The sound of approaching footsteps finally broke them apart. Mia stood flushed and unsteady on her feet before him, her eyes lowering from the heat and fire still burning in his.

'We should press on,' Bryn said, stepping back from her. 'There are other people heading our way. We can finish this later.'

The promise in his words left her breathless with fevered anticipation as she tried to get her legs to follow where he was leading. All her reasons for resisting him were being obliterated by her need to feel his mouth on hers again. She craved to feel his hands on her body—all of her body—his caressing touch preparing her for the most thrilling intimacy of all. She could almost feel his hard, thick presence between her thighs as she tried to negotiate the uneven path on her increasingly unsteady legs. A pulse was still beating deep inside her, made all the more insistent when she fell into step behind him as the length of his long, muscled legs and firm buttocks kept reminding her of how very male he was and how he affected her in a way no man had ever done before.

They passed a few other hikers and just when she thought she would pass out from a combination of the heat of the sun and the burning desire he had activated, he indicated the path down to Alexandria Bay. 'Fancy a quick swim to cool off?'

She looked at the sparkling blue water of the

bay and sighed with relief. 'I can think of nothing better.'

They made their way down the path to the beach, where the waves were crashing against the shore. They weren't the only people on the beach but it took Mia a moment to realise the other sun-seekers weren't wearing bathers.

'Uh-oh,' she said, quickly turning her back.

'What's wrong?' Bryn asked as he heeled himself out of his trainers.

'Those people...' She indicated with a quick flap of her hand behind her and whispered in an undertone, *'They're naked.'*

'I know.'

'You know?'

'Of course,' he said, stripping himself of his board shorts and tossing them to the sand at his feet. 'This is an officially recognised naturist beach.'

She forced her gaze upwards with an effort. 'I'm not taking my clothes off.'

'You don't have to if you don't want to.' He strode off towards the surf while she was still standing there open-mouthed at the taut line of his back and buttocks.

She watched as he entered the turbulent water, cutting through it effortlessly as he swam out beyond the breakers, his broad, tanned back glistening in the sun.

She sucked in a ragged breath as the sun beat down on her, rivulets of perspiration trickling down between her breasts and thighs. The thought of dispensing with her shorts and top and even her skimpy bikini was suddenly very tempting. It wasn't as if she hadn't skinny-dipped before. Of course, skinny-dipping when you were with a group of girlfriends at a twelfth birthday party, at the dead of night in a small backyard pool when there wasn't a male in sight wasn't quite in the same league as this, but maybe she needed to show Bryn she wasn't the uptight little virginal prude he thought she was.

She stripped off her shorts and flung her T-shirt to the sand and with a deep breath reached behind her to untie her bikini top. She watched as it fell in a little heap on the sand and with another deep breath her hands went to her hips and tugged downwards...

CHAPTER TWELVE

THE water was like chilled champagne against her hot, sticky skin, the turbulent waves breaking over her like thousands of tiny, effervescent bubbles. The wildness of it was exhilarating and so too was the thought that nothing separated her from the feel of the ocean's deep, rhythmic pulse on her body. Her bikini was hardly what anyone would have described as conservative, but bathing without the barrier of fabric was intensely sensual, especially knowing that Bryn was only a few metres away, and the same water that was moving against and over her body was touching him as well.

She caught sight of him diving under a wave before resurfacing to swim out a bit further, his strong, muscled body making light work of the powerful surf.

Mia was a confident and competent swimmer but she could already feel the heavy undertow dragging at her legs and decided against joining him. She body-surfed a few smaller waves before making her way back to her things on the sand, relieved to see the other people had moved further along the beach.

Once she was back in her bikini she sat watching the pounding surf, her thoughts drifting to her earlier conversation with Bryn. His shock announcement about their marriage continuing for an unspecified period of time had thrown her completely. He had made his motives very clear; he wanted her—but for how long? He hadn't put an exact time frame on it, probably because he couldn't see their relationship lasting longer than a week or two; a month if she was lucky. He would no doubt slake his lust for her and within weeks she would be left with nothing but the memories and heartbreak.

She frowned as she thought about his past, how losing his parents so young had made him wary of committing himself emotionally, as his great-aunt had indicated the day Mia had visited her.

Would it be possible to remove the armour

from around his heart? Was she in fact the special woman Agnes Dwyer already believed her to be?

She suppressed a deep sigh of remorse over the deception she had been complicit in. She had always hated all forms of deceit, it went against everything she'd been taught. And certainly lying to an old lady seemed particularly immoral, but what if she could change that right now? All she had to do was agree to make their marriage a real one. The lies she'd told her parents and sisters would no longer be lies. What had begun as a lie would now be the truth. She loved him and, while he was uncertain about his feelings for her, perhaps in time she could teach him that loving someone wasn't always painful and unpredictable.

She watched as he came out of the water to join her, his tall naked body making her breath hitch in her throat. How could she have ever thought she would be able to resist him?

'Did you enjoy your swim?' he asked, showering her with droplets of sea water as he sat down next to her on the sand.

She kept her gaze averted and toyed with the sand near her toes. 'Yes, I did.'

He brushed one finger along the heightened colour of her cheek. 'You're blushing.'

'I'm not used to sitting next to naked men.'

He lay back on the sand and closed his eyes against the glare of the sun. 'You never know, you might get used to it in time.'

Mia sneaked a look at him, her belly doing a little flip-flop all over again. His abdominal muscles were sculptured to perfection; they were like tight rods of steel under the smooth tanned skin, the sprinkling of masculine dark hair that spread from his belly button over his pelvis and down his long strong legs making her skin crawl with the need to feel it rasping against her smoother softness.

He opened one eye and caught her staring at him but before she could turn away he caught her hand and brought it to his chest. She could feel the deep thud of his heart beneath her palm and her own heart started to race when he began to move her hand downwards.

'What are you doing?' she gasped and tried to jerk away.

He held her firm, his gaze locking with hers. 'I want you to feel what you do to me.'

She swallowed as her palm came over his growing hardness, the feel of him swelling beneath her tentative touch making her stomach flutter and her legs go weak. She heard him suck in a sharp breath as she began to explore him and another wave of deep longing rushed through her. His erection was like satin-covered steel, the pulsing heat in her hands making her feel powerful in a way she had never felt before. She looked down at him encased in her slim fingers, the latent power of his body totally under her command. She saw the tiny, pearly bead of moisture starting to pool at the head and her entire body shivered with a thousand tickling fingers of desire.

He let out another deep groan, removed her hand and brought it above her head as he turned her on her back so he could lean over her, his head blocking the sun as his lips found hers.

It was a deeply sensual kiss, unhurried, lazy almost, but no less enthralling. Mia could feel the delicious tension building in her body, the sun's warm rays on her legs and arms making her feel increasingly uninhibited as she responded to each slow-moving glide of his tongue against hers. She sighed with pleasure when he released her bikini top, his warm hand taking the weight of her breast, his thumb rolling over the already puckering nipple.

He lifted his mouth from hers to kiss his way down her neck to each breast, his lips and tongue inciting her desire for him to an almost unbearable level. He suckled and kissed each breast in turn, his teeth grazing her sensitised flesh, making her wriggle until she was beneath him properly, the pressure of his weight as his legs entrapped hers in a steely embrace sending her senses skyrocketing. His erection probed against the barrier of her bikini bottoms, the sensation of him being so intimately close but blocked by just a tiny scrap of fabric making her want him all the more.

His mouth left her breast and his eyes came back to hers, their dark blue depths smouldering with pent-up need. 'We can't do this here, sweetheart.'

Mia blinked up at him. 'W-we can't?'

His mouth twisted ruefully. 'This is a public beach and even though it's practically deserted I don't happen to have a condom on me right now.'

'Oh...'

He tipped up her chin and pressed another hot, lingering kiss to her lips. 'Let's go back to the house and begin our honeymoon properly.' He saw the tiny flicker of doubt come and go in her eyes and added softly, 'That's if you want to. The decision is yours, Mia. If you don't feel ready then that's fine.'

Mia held his gaze, finally realising now she'd never really had a chance in refusing him. She wanted him so much she wasn't sure how she was going to make the journey back to his house, her limbs felt so weak with her need of him. She was surprised he couldn't see her love for him shining from her eyes every time they came in contact with his.

'I want you to make love to me,' she said on a husky whisper of sound.

His eyes were unwavering on hers. 'Are you sure?'

'Yes.'

He got to his feet and offered her a hand, pulling her up to stand in front of him. He didn't say anything, just stood looking down at her up-tilted face for what seemed a very long time.

Mia wondered if he was inwardly gloating

about her acquiescence but if he was there was no sign of it on his face. After a moment he appeared to give himself a mental shake and stepped away to pick up his board shorts, dusting the sand off his body before he put them back on and then rolling up the towel they'd been lying on.

She picked up her bikini top and once she was dressed fell into step beside him as they returned to the path that led the way back.

They walked in silence for most of the way. Mia was aware of Bryn's hand reaching for hers now and again when the width of the path allowed it, but apart from the occasional comment about the view or wildlife he seemed to be preoccupied with his own thoughts.

When the house finally came into view he suggested she have a shower while he made them both some lunch.

She looked at him in uncertainty. 'But I thought you wanted to…you know…'

'I do,' he said and pushed the door open for her. 'But you've had nothing but a few mouthfuls of fruit and water all day. I don't want you fainting on me.'

She was conscious of his gaze following her up

the stairs and turned to look at him when she got to the landing.

'Mia?'

'Yes?'

He seemed about to say something then changed his mind. 'It doesn't matter. Go and have your shower. We can talk later.'

She gave him a tremulous smile and went into the bathroom.

When she came downstairs half an hour later Bryn had also showered and changed into shorts and a T-shirt. He looked up from the salad and cheese and cold-meat platter he was assembling as she came into the kitchen. 'Would you like a glass of wine?'

'Sure, why not?'

He handed her two glasses of chilled white wine. 'Take those out to the deck and I'll bring our lunch out.'

The deck was set amongst the trees and over-looked the pool and lower garden. Some rainbow lorikeets were jostling just a few feet away and Mia began hunting the upper limbs of the trees for any sign of koalas.

'Have you found any?' Bryn asked as he set the lunch platter down on the table.

'Not as yet,' she said, reaching for her wine. She took a tiny sip and let out a breath of delight. 'This is such a lovely setting. It feels as if the bush is an extension of the house.'

He smiled and took the seat opposite, lifting his glass to hers. 'What shall we drink to?'

'Dutch courage?' she suggested after a moment.

His expression softened as he held her gaze. 'Don't be nervous, Mia. I won't hurt you. I promise.'

She gave her bottom lip a little nibble and then, releasing it, confessed, 'I can't help it.'

He put down his glass and reached for her hand, his fingers strong but gentle as they entwined with hers. 'Trust me, Mia. I know what I'm doing.'

'I know this is stupid but I can't help thinking I'll disappoint you. You've had millions of lovers. What if I don't...you know...satisfy you?'

'Not quite millions,' he said, smiling at her little furrowed brow. 'How could you ever think that you won't satisfy me? You're so damned sexy I can barely keep my hands off you. I know you and I are going to be dynamite together. I can feel it every time you touch me. I was ready to explode on that beach with your soft little fingers crawling all over me.'

Mia felt a warm glow at his words. Never had a man made her feel more like a woman. He only had to look at her with those dark blue eyes and her flesh began to tingle all over. The thought of him possessing her thrilled her until she could barely sit still on the seat.

He took another sip of wine, his gaze thoughtful and steady on hers. 'I still find it hard to believe you haven't had a lover before now.'

She pushed at a bit of salad with her fork. 'When I was seventeen a close friend of mine contracted a sexually transmitted disease. It was so awful for her. To make matters worse the boy who gave it to her blamed her and started spreading rumours. In the end she had to change schools.' She gave a little sigh and added, 'I guess I've always been a little bit afraid of getting hurt since then.'

He reached for her hand, his long fingers interlinking with hers. 'I have always practised safe sex. I absolutely insist on it no matter what the circumstances. It's not fair on either partner to be landed with a disease or a pregnancy that wasn't planned, not that accidents don't happen, of course, but at least there are ways to deal with it these days.'

'If an accident did happen...' she stared down at the table in front of her rather than meet his eyes '...what would you expect me to do about it?'

He thought about it for a moment and in the end didn't answer her question but asked one of his own. 'What would you want to do?'

'I guess you can already tell I've had a pretty conservative upbringing,' she said. 'There are no doubt circumstances when a termination seems like the only option, but having an adopted sister has made me realise that even if a baby is unwanted by its natural parent or parents there are plenty of other people who do want it and would love it as dearly as their own.'

Bryn sat in silence, thinking about the gentle, loving wisdom behind her convictions.

'But don't worry,' she added with a little upwards glance before looking down again to re-arrange the food on her plate, 'I'm on a low-dose

Pill to regulate my cycle. There won't be any little accidents.'

'If there were I would not expect you to do anything you weren't comfortable doing,' he said. 'I would support you through whatever decision you felt was appropriate.'

She brought her gaze back up to his, surprised by his sincerity. 'Thank you.'

He sat watching her playing with her food, his own meal barely touched.

'You're not eating,' he said after a short, throbbing silence.

'I'm not all that hungry for some reason…'

'I am,' he said, his dark eyes glittering with desire. 'But not for food.'

He got to his feet and came around to where she was sitting, and, taking her hand, in his brought her to her feet. He bent his head and kissed her deeply, the rasp of his skin against the softness of hers making her tingle all over with fevered longing.

By the time they got to his bedroom Mia was breathless with anticipation, every nerve and pulse leaping under her skin in growing excitement. Tension crackled in the air as he closed the door and came towards her, his hands gently removing her sarong from around her chest. She felt the soft-as-air fabric glide down her body to land in a circle at her feet.

His eyes ran over her naked breasts before he cupped their light weight in his hands. She could hardly breathe with him so close, the pulse of his aroused body pressing against her.

He released her briefly to tug his T-shirt over his head, tossing it to one side as he stepped out of his shorts and briefs. She gave a tiny swallow as he came back to her, his fingers untying the strings that held her bikini bottoms in place.

Without a word he lifted her in his arms and carried her to the white expanse of the bed, laying her down before joining her, his weight balanced by his arms.

His mouth found hers, softly at first and then with increasing pressure, taking her on a sensual journey that totally captivated her. His mouth moved from hers to scorch a pathway to her breasts, the hot lave of his tongue turning her insides to liquid heat. He travelled lower, exploring the dip of her belly button before his warm breath feathered over the tiny landing strip of soft, dark blonde, closely cropped curls that shielded her femininity. With the gentlest touch possible he parted her delicate folds before tasting her with his mouth. The sensation of his tongue against her arched her back and made her whimper in intense pleasure, her hands clutching at his shoulders.

'Relax for me, baby,' he coached her softly. 'Let yourself go.'

'I can't...'

'Yes, you can,' he said. 'I want to pleasure you.'

'But I want you to...to...be inside me.'

He moved back up her body with slow but exquisite caresses, building her need of him to fever pitch. Each stroke of his hands along the flanks of her thighs, each hot, moist kiss to the indentation of her waist and each tender suckle on her breasts made her nearly mad with the need for more. Just when she thought she could stand it no longer he reached between her legs, gently easing her apart to insert one finger, waiting until she was comfortable before deepening his tender stroke, the silky dew of her desire making it easier and easier for her to accept him further.

'Oh, God…' she breathed, writhing beneath his touch.

'You feel so warm and wet,' he said, his voice low and deep, his breath like a caress on her skin. 'You're so ready for me.'

He leaned across her to the bedside drawer and took out a condom. She watched with bated breath as he applied it, coming back to position himself over her.

'Tell me to stop if it hurts.'

'I will…'

He moved against her, parting her to take him partially, waiting for her to accommodate him before going further.

'Are you OK?' he asked.

'Yes…'

He hesitated. 'Are you sure?'

'I'm sure…'

He moved slowly, holding back as her tight body wrapped itself around him. He felt her flinch and stalled again. 'Did that hurt?'

'No…not really.'

'God, Mia,' he groaned and began to withdraw. 'I wish I could do this but I can't bear to hurt you.'

Mia clutched at him to hold him in place.

'You're not hurting me; I like it. I like the feel of you. Please don't stop.' She saw his throat move up and down as he looked at her. 'Please, Bryn, I want this. I want you to make love to me.'

Bryn hesitated but she lifted her hips against him and he was lost as he surged against her, sheathing himself in the tight, moist cocoon of her body. He tried to move slowly but she wouldn't allow it, her hands digging into his buttocks to increase his pace. He fought to keep control but she was urging him on, her panting little cries of pleasure as he thrust deeper and deeper making his heart contract with totally unfamiliar feelings. He shifted position so she could feel him more intensely, caressing her with his fingers to take her to the summit with him so he could feel the contractions of her orgasm to finally push him over the edge. He could feel the pulse of her body as it built in arousal, her slim limbs wrapping around him, holding on tight for the rapidly approaching storm of sensation that threatened to burst at any moment.

Suddenly she was there, her high, keening cry of ecstasy washing over him as she convulsed against him, triggering his own release with an explosion of pleasure that lifted the hair on his scalp with its breathtaking force.

'Oh, wow…'she said on an expelled breath as her heart rate began to lower.

He dragged himself off her chest, where he'd collapsed, to smile down at her radiant face. 'Oh, wow?'

She returned his smile, two tiny dimples appearing either side of her mouth. 'Definitely oh, wow.'

'I didn't hurt you?'

'Not much.'

He frowned. 'I wanted to take things slowly. I didn't want to cause you any pain.'

'I'm fine, Bryn,' she reassured him. 'It was wonderful. You were wonderful. Thank you for being so gentle with me.'

He tucked a tendril of hair behind her ear, his eyes meshing with hers. 'I've never met anyone like you before. It felt different somehow.'

Hope fluttered inside Mia's chest at his unexpected confession. 'How?' she asked, hunting his face for a sign of what he was feeling.

'I've always experienced sex as a physical thing. I've always been able to keep emotions separate.'

'What are you trying to say?'

He released a sigh and pressed a soft kiss to her forehead, lifting his head to look down at her, a small frown bringing his brows almost together. 'I have no idea.'

She frowned as he lifted himself away. He was pulling away from her again. She could feel the barriers come up as if their intimacy had affected him more than he wanted to admit, to her certainly, but even, it seemed, to himself.

'Bryn?'

He turned back to look at her, his expression now stripped of all emotion. 'Sorry, Mia, I know this is the part where women like you expect a declaration of love, but I can't give it to you. I'd like to but I can't. It wouldn't be fair to you. I'm sorry.'

Mia felt as if someone had ripped open her chest and stomped heavily on her heart. 'I'm not looking for that from you,' she lied. 'I understand the terms of our relationship.'

He held her gaze for a lengthy moment. 'You deserve much better than me, Mia. You really do.'

She opened her mouth to respond but he turned and left the room, closing the door behind him.

She flopped back on the pillows in sinking despair. How would she ever find a way to his heart?

CHAPTER THIRTEEN

IT WAS early evening before Mia saw him again. When she'd come downstairs he had already cleared the abandoned lunch things away and a brief note propped on the bench informed her he had gone back to the beach for a surf.

He came into the lounge just as she was leaving it, almost colliding with her in the doorway. He steadied her with his hands, looking down at her as if seeing her for the first time.

'Sorry,' she said. 'I didn't hear you come in.'

His gaze dipped to her mouth for a moment before returning to her grey eyes. His hands fell away from her shoulders and he moved further into the room, a hand making a rough pathway through his already disordered hair.

'Are you OK?' Mia asked.

He gave her a twisted smile as he turned to face her. 'I think I might have had too much sun.'

'Would you like me to get you some water?'

'No, I don't need water. I need my head read, that's what I need.'

She wasn't sure what to make of his mood. She stood in front of him uncertainly, beginning to worry her bottom lip with her teeth.

'Damn it, I wish you would stop doing that!' he said roughly.

She blinked at him in surprise. 'Stop doing what?'

'Everything.'

She frowned in confusion. 'Everything?'

He let out his breath in a stream. 'God, I must have been crazy that day. I should have known something like this would happen.' He sent his fingers through his sand-encrusted hair.

'What are you talking about?' she asked. 'Wh-what's happened?'

His eyes cut back to hers. 'Everything you do gets to me. Every look, every smile, and every word you say. It all gets to me.'

She lowered her eyes. 'I'm sorry…'

He stepped closer and forced her chin up to

hold his gaze. 'I have spent most of the years of my life avoiding the complication of emotional entanglements and in one brief meeting with a feisty little fitness fanatic all my defences get knocked down.'

Mia stared at him speechlessly, her heart beginning to ram against her sternum. What was he saying? That he loved her after all? Hope began to flicker in her chest, the tiny, frantic, flapping wings of it making it hard for her to breathe properly.

'I promised myself I wouldn't touch you again after this afternoon,' he went on. 'It was wrong to touch you in the first place but I just couldn't seem to help myself. From the moment I met you I wanted you. I still want you but I can't give you what you deserve, what you've been brought up to expect, what is your right as a lovely young woman with a generous heart. You need someone with the capacity to love. I'm not that person.'

'How do you know you're not?' she asked.

'Mia, listen to me.' His hands tightened on her shoulders, the gravity of his expression unnerving her totally. 'I've never told this to anyone before.' He took a ragged breath and continued, 'Do you know what the last thing I said to my mother was the night she and my father were killed?'

She shook her head, tears starting to sprout in her eyes, her bottom lip trembling.

'They were going out to dinner together. My father was already in the car but my mother had turned back to give me one last cuddle. I told her I loved her.' His voice cracked over the words. 'I don't think I had ever said it before. I told her to tell my father I loved him too.'

'Oh, Bryn…' She choked back a sob.

'When the police came to our house where I was being looked after by a babysitter my whole world collapsed. If I hadn't called my mother back at that moment she and my father would still be alive. But I called her back and those few precious seconds it took to tell her I loved her cost her and my father their lives. I taught myself not to feel from that moment. It's like a switch was turned off inside me and I can no longer find where it is.'

'You just need to give yourself time… Your great-aunt's health is bringing it all back up for you. You're still grieving…you haven't dealt with the past and it's coming back to haunt you.'

'I don't want to deal with the past!' He threw the

words at her as he released her almost savagely. 'It won't change a thing rehashing it all now.'

'But it won't go away just because you choose to ignore it. It will plague you all your life. You'll end up a lonely old man with nothing to show for your life. No fulfilling relationships, no children to love you.'

'I would hate any child of mine to go through what I did. It's just not worth the risk. Losing a parent is the most devastating thing that can happen to a child. Losing both of them in one fell swoop is beyond anything I can describe.'

'It might not happen. Just because you lost your parents in a tragic accident doesn't mean history will repeat itself.'

'Mia, you are the sweetest, most adorable person I've ever met,' he said, taking her by the shoulders again. 'If there was anyone I would be able to love, it is you. But I can't pretend to feel what is just not there.'

She let the tears fall unheeded, touched by his honesty in a way no one had ever touched her before. 'I love you enough for both of us... I thought I hated you at first but somehow it all changed, and I can't turn it off.'

He gave her one of his twisted smiles. 'We're an odd couple, aren't we? You have too much love to give and I don't have any.'

'You do but you can't recognise it,' she said. 'You won't allow yourself to become vulnerable but that's what life is all about. You hide your feelings behind a façade of biting cynicism, taking pot-shots at whoever comes across your path. Your public reputation is built on that but I know now it isn't really who you are as a person. Inside is a deeply sensitive, caring man who is just too afraid to love again in case it gets snatched away.'

'I can't give you what you want. I know I can't.'

'I haven't even told you what I want, so how can you say that?'

He let out a sigh and rested his chin on the top of her head. 'What do you want, Mia?'

She hugged him to her in a desperate effort to get close to him. 'I want you. Only you. For as long as you'll have me.'

He eased her away from him to look deep into her tear-washed eyes. 'You're prepared to risk being hurt by me?'

'I'm prepared to be vulnerable because that's what love is all about.'

'Even if I can never find that switch inside of me?'

She linked her arms around his neck and brought his mouth down to hers. 'Don't worry, I'll find it. You've just been looking in all the wrong places.'

Her lips were so soft and yielding he had no choice but to respond even though his common sense told him to let her go before he damaged her permanently. He sank into her warmth, his arms tightening around her, fighting for the control he had always taken for granted in the past. Something about Mia touched him where no one else had ever been. He couldn't put his finger on exactly what it was but he felt as if she lightened the load he had been carrying for so long.

He pushed her back towards the sofa, his hands going to her sarong, releasing it so he could suckle on her small but perfect breasts. Her little gasps of delight released a trickle of sensation deep inside him; she was so responsive to his touch, as if she had been waiting for him all this time.

He carried her to the bedroom, laying her down only long enough to get a condom. She writhed against him, wanting more and he gave it unreservedly. He dispensed with the rest of her clothes and sank into her with a single thrust that he should have checked but somehow couldn't. She welcomed him with silky moistness, the delicate fragrance of her need filling his nostrils. He drove a little harder, hoping she wasn't still tender from earlier but unable to pull back the pace. He could feel the pressure building around him, hers mingling with his in an erotic pulse that grew more frantic by the second. He struggled to hold back but she was with him all the way, arching her back to receive each deep surge of his body, her gasping cries like a haunting tune he had been searching for all his life but never found until this moment. She went soaring a few moments ahead of him, the tight clench of her feminine form leaving him no choice but to follow in a rush of feeling that threatened to overwhelm him. He felt the explosion of his life force within her, the emptying of himself beyond anything he had ever experienced before.

It was a long time before he could find the strength to speak and the only thing he could think of to say was, 'Oh, wow…'

Mia smiled up at him. 'Oh, wow?'

He kissed the tip of her nose. 'You are very definitely an "oh, wow" sort of lover.'

Even though you don't love me, Mia thought sadly.

Bryn brought her close, tucking her head against his chest, his fingers splaying through her hair, wondering if he could ever find the words to tell her what he had done to bring about their relationship. His immediate lust for her had overridden every other consideration; he had not stopped to weigh up the cost if she in the end proved to be someone very special.

And very special she was.

In a way he had never expected.

He had not thought it possible to trust life enough to care for someone unreservedly, but somehow Mia had invaded his emotional firewall, finding a way to his heart that no one had ever done before.

He had told her bluntly and rather clinically he could not offer her a declaration of love but what if what she'd said was true? That he was unable to recognise his true feelings for fear of life hurting him the way it had in the past?

He had definitely felt something from the very first moment he'd met her—her sparkling defiance had got his notice, but so too had her spirit and her big heart, not to mention her passion and zest for life. Every time she looked up at him with her beautiful, elfin face with those big grey eyes he felt that tiny fish-hook tug on him deep inside his chest. Was that love, the sort of love that could last a lifetime?

In spite of her dislike for him she had agreed to marry him for the sake of his great-aunt. She hadn't done it for the money; she had done it out of the kindness of her heart. She gave of herself so generously, laying herself bare for him even though he had offered her nothing in terms of emotional commitment.

He recalled all the bitter mornings-after he'd endured in the past; women who had wanted much more than he'd been prepared to give, one even stalking him relentlessly, making his life unbearable for a time.

Mia, on the other hand, was a young woman who was prepared to love him unconditionally. She'd agreed to his conditions and with grace and dignity accepted them.

He wished he could be truly honest with her but the thought of her finding out how he had engineered their marriage made him baulk. How on earth could he frame the words in any way that would make them less offensive to her? He had swept her career out of his way with a sleight of hand that was no less than despicable.

He was still thinking about how best to make it up to her when his mobile phone rang. He kept Mia close to him, his hand on the back of her silky head as he reached for it, the voice on the other end informing him of the one thing he had been dreading and yet preparing himself for over the last few months.

'What's wrong?' Mia asked as he put the phone down a few seconds later.

His voice was flat and emotionless as he informed her, 'My great-aunt slipped into a coma a short time ago. She's not expected to come out of it.'

Her face fell, sending yet another dagger to his heart. 'Oh, no…'

'We'll have to fly back in the morning,' he said, moving away before she could reach for him to offer comfort. It didn't seem right to be accepting her comfort when she had no idea of how he had acted. He felt tainted with it, hating himself, hating his vulnerability where she was concerned. Hating that life yet again was letting him down and there was nothing he could do to stop it.

'Bryn…I'm so sorry… Is there anything I can do?'

'No,' he said, a shutter seeming to come down over his features as he faced her. 'I'll re-book the flights on line. You go to bed. You look tired.'

'But I'm not tired,' Mia insisted. 'I want to be with you to help you through this.'

'I don't want company right now.' He turned to look out of the window. 'Please leave me to deal with this on my own.'

'I don't think you should be alone at a time like this,' she said softly. 'I want to support you and—'

'Didn't you hear what I said?' He swung around to glare at her. 'I said, I want to be alone.'

Mia stood her ground, even though her legs were quaking at the burning glitter in his eyes. 'You can't push me away. I want to be with you. I love you. This is what love is about, supporting and helping when things are tough.'

'Leave me alone, damn you!' He grabbed her by the arm and led her to the door, almost shoving her through. 'I don't need you. I don't need anyone.'

The door slammed in her face and her shoulders slumped in defeat. She heard the sound of a glass smashing against the wall and then nothing but silence. An empty, aching silence that tore at her heart for what he was going through.

Alone.

She went upstairs and, going to his room, quietly packed his bag before going to do her own. She sat on the edge of her bed and stared at her hands where his rings encircled her finger.

It would soon be over.

He didn't need her any more.

His great-aunt was close to death so the final curtain would soon be coming down on their act. In spite of what he'd said about continuing their relationship for a period of time she knew their temporary marriage was now coming to an end.

Bryn barely spoke to her on the way back to Sydney the next morning. He sat staring out of the window for the entire flight, even ignoring the air steward's offer of refreshments.

After they collected their baggage they drove in silence to the palliative-care unit. Mia glanced at him several times but his face was set in the same impenetrable mask, no hint of emotion showing.

Agnes was lying like a thin shadow on the bed, her chest rising and falling so slowly it looked as if she was hardly breathing at all.

The doctor spoke to Bryn in an office further down the hall while Mia sat by the bedside, holding the thin, papery hand and wishing with all her heart she could make things right for both of them.

When Bryn came back she gave up her seat for him so he could be near his great-aunt. He gave her the flicker of a grateful smile and sat down, reaching for the limp hand on the bed.

Mia stood behind him, gently massaging his shoulders as he leaned forward in the chair, his voice low and deep as he spoke to his great-aunt. 'I'm here, Aunt Aggie. Mia and I are here.'

The day passed slowly, the clock on the wall measuring time as if heavy weights were attached to its hands, each minute crawling by, each hour turning over like a month instead of sixty minutes.

* * *

There was no change in Agnes's condition over the next five days. Bryn spent as much time at the hospital as he could, sitting by his great-aunt's bedside until it was time to broadcast his radio show. While he was on air Mia sat by the bedside, stroking the thin hand of his great-aunt, listening to the radio playing softly in the background, amazed at how normal and unaffected Bryn seemed. The show must go on, she thought as she watched the shallow rise and fall of his dying relative's chest. No one would ever know what he was dealing with in his private life. His lively banter with the people he interviewed and the upbeat music he played gave no clue to the grief he was privately preparing himself for. He spoke of their honeymoon as if it had been the most wonderful experience of his life and yet she knew it was all an act, for he had no such feelings for her. At least he had been totally honest with her. So many men wouldn't have been. How many times had previous boyfriends declared their undying affection for her, only to walk away without a backward glance when she refused to sleep with them?

No, at least Bryn had been honest from the word go. He had told her he needed her to act the role of his fiancée and wife for his great-aunt's benefit as well as his ratings. He hadn't pretended anything he didn't feel and, even though it was heartbreakingly disappointing, in a way she was grateful he had been so up-front about it. If only she had more time to let her love for him heal the hurt he'd carried for so long, maybe then he would open up to the possibility of a permanent future together.

'How is she?' Bryn asked softly when he came in later that evening.

Mia made room beside the bed for him. 'The doctor was in a while ago,' she said, swallowing back the emotion. 'It's not looking good, Bryn. He doesn't think it will be long now.'

He placed his hand against the nape of her neck, his warm palm easing the stiffness that had gathered there from sitting so long. 'Why don't you go home and get some sleep? You've been here for hours.'

'I'm fine…I just didn't want her to be alone…'

'I'm here now,' he said. 'I'll call Henry to take you home.'

'No, please, let me stay,' she said, looking up at him. 'Please?'

His hand came around from her nape to gently cradle her cheek, his thumb stroking the creamy softness as he looked into her shining with moisture eyes. 'You really do love me, don't you?'

She gave him a wobbly smile. 'Yes…I do.'

There was a long, intense pause as he held her gaze.

'Mia,' he said, stopping to clear his throat. 'There's something I need to tell you—'

There was a sudden beeping from the monitor attached to Agnes's chest, signalling her heart was failing.

Two nurses and a doctor came rushing in but there was nothing they could do.

Agnes Gabriella Dwyer died at seven twenty-three that evening with both Bryn and Mia by her bedside. It was a peaceful passing and Mia was glad the old woman had not died alone. She found it impossible not to cry but did so as quietly as she could, knowing it would be hard on Bryn, who was clearly fighting to maintain control. She saw the up and down movement of his throat and the tight clench of his hands when he finally moved away from the bed to discuss arrangements with the staff over his great-aunt's personal belongings.

It was late by the time they left to go back to his house and Mia could see the lines of exhaustion around his eyes as he opened the car door for her.

'I can drive if you're too tired,' she offered.

He gave her another on-off smile touched with sadness. 'No, I'm fine. It's a short drive anyway.'

He waited until they were parked in the garage before he spoke again. He switched off the engine and turned in his seat to face her. 'Thank you for what you did this week.'

'I didn't do anything…'

He captured a strand of her hair and tucked it behind her ear, the gesture so tender she felt more tears springing to her eyes.

'Yes, you did,' he said, his voice sounding as if it had been dragged across something rough. 'You supported me through a tough time. I can't imagine how I would have coped without you.'

'I'm so sorry about your great-aunt…' she said, stroking the hand that had come up to cup her cheek.

'She died happily and peacefully because of

you. I couldn't have achieved that for her without your help.'

'I'm glad you asked me to help.'

He looked at her for a long time without speaking. Mia could hear the faint ticking of the dashboard clock and the squeak of leather as he shifted marginally in his seat.

The pad of his thumb moved over her bottom lip, his eyes growing darker as they meshed with hers. 'I want you, Mia.'

'I want you too,' she said softly.

He unfolded himself from his seat and came around to her side, helping her out on legs that felt weak and unsteady. He slipped an arm around her shoulders and walked with her into the house, shutting the door behind him and giving her a look burning with such sensual promise she felt as if she was melting on the spot.

'Come here,' he commanded.

She stepped into his arms, her mouth connecting with his in a fiery kiss that spoke of deep mutual longings. He broke the kiss to carry her upstairs, looking down at her with smouldering heat as he placed her on the bed. She watched as he removed his clothes, her pulse leaping at the sight of how very aroused he already was. She began to fumble with her own clothing but wasn't getting very far until he came down over her and helped.

His hands moved over her breasts, his mouth anointing them with hot, wet kisses and suckles that curled her toes and arched her back. He went lower and lower until she felt the flicker of his tongue against her dewy feminine heat, the sensations rippling through her at this most intimate of all caresses. The pleasure he evoked was mind-blowing and totally unstoppable. It hit her like a huge wave crashing against the shore, lifting her, rolling her over and over before tossing her down once more to float in a sea of euphoria.

He moved back up and, leaning across her, rummaged for a condom, putting it on before slipping between her parted thighs. He entered her in a single deep thrust that sent her back against the pillows with a gasp of delight as he filled her completely. He set a hectic, breathless pace and she got carried along with it, relishing the feel of his pulsing need. She felt him briefly tense before his final plunge, and then his deep groan of satisfaction as he emptied himself, the aftershocks of his release triggering little shivers of pleasure all over her skin.

She held him to her, listening as his breathing gradually came back to normal, his chest rising and falling against hers as she stroked his back with her fingers. How would she live without this when he called an end to their relationship?

So many times over the last few days she'd caught him looking at her when he thought she wasn't aware of it, frowning slightly, as if he couldn't make up his mind about her. Even as they'd sat beside his great-aunt's bed he had seemed on the brink of saying something important. What had he been about to say to her? she wondered. Had he been mentally preparing his announcement that their temporary marriage was coming to a close?

But then, as she considered another possibility, she felt a tickling sensation inside her chest, as if a tiny feather residing there had been lifted by a gentle breeze of hope.

What if he had been trying to tell her he loved her?

She took a small breath, her fingers stilling on his back. 'Bryn...'

'Mmm…'

'You were going to say something just before…before your great aunt passed away.' She eased him off her so she could look into his eyes. 'What was it you were going to tell me?'

He held her gaze without speaking for what seemed an age before he got off the bed and reached for his trousers, turning his back as he got dressed.

'Bryn?' She sat up, her stomach hollowing as she felt his barriers come up. 'You said it was something important.'

'It wasn't.' His tone was curt as he turned to face her, his face an expressionless mask. 'I have some phone calls to make in regards to the funeral arrangements.'

She glanced at the clock and frowned. 'At this time of night?'

He didn't answer but left the room, closing the door with a sharp click behind him.

Mia lay back on the pillows with a sigh. Was this how it was going to be between them, her love trying desperately to reach out to him, while he kept pushing it away?

CHAPTER FOURTEEN

THE funeral was a private one and Mia thought how well Bryn coped with it, considering the pain she knew he was feeling. For the days leading up to the memorial service she had been aware of him keeping his distance, reminding her of an injured animal that didn't want anyone else to see its true vulnerability as it dealt with its wounds in private. The only place he let his guard slip was in bed at night. She treasured those times when he rocked and shuddered in her arms, his body finally relaxing as he spilled himself, his iron-clad control slipping as he took her with him to paradise.

She woke one morning a week after the funeral to find him watching her, his dark blue eyes steady and thoughtful on hers.

'Hi...' she said, lifting a fingertip to his lips, tracing them lovingly.

He captured her hand and kissed her fingertip, making her flesh tingle anew at the passion she had felt last night in his arms. He had taken her on a sensual journey that had known no limits. Her body still throbbed tenderly where he had driven so hard, as if he had wanted to demonstrate his desire for her in the most primitive way possible. He hadn't even bothered with using a condom, his passion so out of control as he had taken her from behind, causing a catastrophic explosion of ecstasy that had left her totally boneless.

'What are you thinking?' she asked after a long, pulsing silence.

He gave a rueful grimace. 'I wonder how many men are being asked exactly that question all over the world right now.'

She tried to smile but something about his expression unnerved her, making her lips twist unevenly instead. 'I know, but I guess women like to know what's going on in men's minds. You always seem to hide it so well.'

A small frown brought his brows even closer. His fingers picked up a strand of her hair and coiled it absently, his dark gaze for once not quite connecting with hers. 'There are things we need to discuss, Mia, now that my great-aunt has gone.'

Mia felt her chest tighten painfully. This was it, she thought with a sinking heart.

Their temporary marriage was over.

She lowered her gaze, staring fixedly at his chest. 'I understand…'

He released her and got out of the bed, reaching for a bathrobe and wrapping around himself before turning to address her in a tone that was distant and detached. 'I have a meeting with my producer and the team this morning so I have to leave soon, but I'd like to have dinner with you tonight so we can talk about where we're going from here.'

She swallowed the thickness of dread in her throat and forced a stiff smile to her lips. 'Where would you like to go to dinner? Do you want me to book somewhere in particular?'

'No, I'll do it. Just be ready by seven-thirty,' he said. 'If I'm going to be late I'll get Henry to pick you up.'

'Whatever.'

His unreadable dark eyes met hers briefly. 'We have to talk, Mia, you know that. Your family will be returning soon and I wouldn't want them to get the wrong idea about us.'

'I know…'

He left the room and the house soon after but it was a long time before she could bring herself to get out of the bed, where the scent of his desire for her wrapped her in a shroud of something that felt like comfort, which she knew would very probably have to last her for the rest of her life.

It was purely by chance Mia ran into Shelley from the café as she was coming back from having her hair done in the city. She'd been filling in time, trying to distract herself from the evening ahead, which she knew would spell the end of her relationship with Bryn.

'Mia…' Shelley gave her an uncomfortable look as they jostled in the doorway of a boutique in the Strand Arcade. 'I was just thinking about you.'

'You were?' Mia frowned at her former workmate's expression.

'How are things with your dream husband?' Shelley asked after a tight little pause. 'Still madly in love?'

'Why wouldn't I be?' she asked guardedly.

Shelley took her by the arm and led her out of the hearing of the other shoppers, waiting until they were in a quiet corner near the stairs to the upper floors. 'Mia, I hate to be the one to tell you this but someone needs to before you get hurt any further.' She took a deep breath and said, 'Your marriage to Bryn Dwyer is a total sham.'

Mia fought to conceal her reaction and asked in a calm, unaffected tone, 'What makes you say that?'

Shelley glanced right and left to make sure no one was listening and lowered her tone even further. 'I overheard a conversation in the café this morning. Bryn was there with your agent, Roberta Askinthorpe. They were looking very cosy.'

Mia felt as if someone had thumped her in the chest. 'Oh really?'

'I hovered about, pretending to be clearing the table behind, and I heard something that I wish I didn't have to tell you but I think you should know.'

Mia fought against the wave of nausea that had risen in her throat. 'Wh-what did you hear?'

'Bryn Dwyer had you dropped from Peach Pie Productions. Theodore Frankston was against it but Bryn insisted. He also had you

removed from your agent's books because he
wanted you to have no choice but to act as his
wife in order to secure his great-aunt's estate.
Apparently her will was written in such a way
that unless she thoroughly approved of his
choice of wife the fortune—and I mean fortune
in capital letters—would be given to the man
who killed his parents.'

Mia stared at her in shock, the blood draining
from her face. 'But no one knows about his
parents…'

'I sort of guessed that, it was the first I'd heard
of it too, but the way Roberta and Bryn were
speaking about it made me realise it must be the
truth. Apparently Bryn's great-aunt felt he should
forgive the man responsible for the death of his
parents. It was her way of ensuring he did something about his life and the way it was heading.

'I'm sorry I had to tell you this,' Shelley went
on awkwardly. 'I just thought you should know.'
She let out a little sigh of empathy. 'Look, I know
you love him—there's hardly a woman in
Sydney who doesn't—but you can't let him do
this to you. He married you for money, Mia. Now
his great-aunt is dead he'll get rid of you. Your

marriage will be over. He doesn't love you. I thought he did, everyone thought he did, but as actors go he surely takes the Oscar. He used you to get what he wanted. He used you despicably and very cruelly.'

'Thank you for telling me.' Somehow Mia found her strangled voice.

Shelley gave her an agonised look. 'I wish I hadn't been there to hear it with my own ears. God, Mia, what will you do?'

She straightened her shoulders, her grey eyes firing up with determination. 'I'm going to do what I'm best at. I'm going to act.'

Shelley frowned. 'Act?'

'You just watch me, Shelley,' Mia said. 'Bryn Dwyer is not going to get away with thinking he can walk all over my career.'

'What about your heart?'

'That too.'

Shelley gave her a doubtful look. 'If you need me at any time, just let me know. He's a bastard, Mia, a total bastard who has no heart.'

'I know,' Mia said through gritted teeth. 'But I'm not letting him have the satisfaction of trampling over mine. If it takes every bit of acting ability I possess I am going to teach him the lesson he should have learned a long time ago.'

'What are you going to do?'

She met her friend's troubled gaze. 'I'm going to get in first, that's what I'm going to do.'

'You mean, pull the plug on your marriage before he gets the chance?'

Mia smiled even though it hurt unbearably. 'I may not be up to scratch on acting the *femme fatale* role according to Bryn Dwyer's opinion, but the one role I can do convincingly is the I-never-loved-you-in-the-first-place one.'

'But you really do love him, don't you?'

'I'm an actor, Shelley,' Mia reminded her. 'And I'm telling you if I can't pull this off then I'm going to give up and go back to college and find some other career.'

'Such as?'

Mia frowned as she thought about it. 'I don't know… maybe working in a café wouldn't be so bad after all.'

Shelley reached out and gave her a quick hug. 'Don't even think about it. You were born to be on stage—you just haven't found the right one yet.'

* * *

Mia had no choice but to tell Gina about the true state of her marriage, for as soon as her former flatmate answered the door Gina could see for herself the emotional despair on her face.

'I can't believe it!' Gina said once Mia had told her everything. 'I thought he was in love with you.'

'He's in love with himself, not me,' Mia said, wiping at her eyes.

'But what if Shelley didn't hear correctly? I mean, a café is hardly a quiet place. There are usually several conversations going on at once and cups and plates rattling in the background,' Gina said. 'Surely you owe Bryn a chance to explain his motivations for marrying you?'

'We're having dinner this evening,' Mia informed her. 'He said this morning before he left that he wanted to discuss our future. That could only mean one thing.'

Gina's face fell. 'Oh...'

'I'm not going to give him the satisfaction of waving the chequered flag in my face. I'm going to ask for a divorce.'

'Your room is still empty,' Gina said. 'You can come back here any time.'

'Thanks, Gina. I'm going back to pack my

bags now. I'll bring them here as soon as I'm done. I just want to tell Bryn Dwyer what I think of him and get it over with.'

'Look what happened the last time you said that,' Gina said wryly. 'It doesn't always pay to go looking for revenge. You're the one who will get hurt.'

Mia scrubbed at her eyes determinedly. 'I'm not going to let him see how much he hurt me. You just wait and see, Gina. This is going to be the performance of my life.'

CHAPTER FIFTEEN

MIA had not long finished packing her things at Bryn's house when she received a phone call from Ellie, who was now safely relaxing with a group of friends on the Greek island of Santorini.

'I can't thank you enough for what you did for me,' Ellie said. 'It was such a harrowing time. I really thought I was going to lose it there for a while. The money you sent helped release fifteen people. You should be very proud of yourself.'

'Yes, well, that's what sisters are for,' she said with a touch of wryness, 'to make sacrifices. You've done it for me lots of times.'

'So how's the gorgeous husband?'

'He's...' Mia hesitated, wondering if she should ruin her sister's well-earned holiday with the news of her impending divorce. 'I'm having dinner with him tonight. I can hardly wait.'

'I'm so happy for you, Mia, you so deserve to be happy. You're always so good at helping others. It's time you got to be treated like a princess. Love you, sis. I'll be home in a couple of weeks and thanks again for not telling the folks about the drama I was in. I knew I could count on you. You're the best.'

'I love you too, Ellie. Don't go saving any whales or forests on your way home. Just come home and be with me, right?'

'It's a deal,' Ellie said.

A short time later another call came through, this time from Mia's previous agent, informing her of a role she thought Mia might be interested in auditioning for.

'But I thought you were too busy to represent me,' Mia said with unmistakable bitterness.

'Yes, well, it's more of a permanent role so it doesn't quite fall into our regular guidelines for representation. I just thought, since you were at a loose end, you might like this. You would be perfect for it.'

'What is it?'

'It's a job working with sick children in hospital. It sounds like a lot of fun and the money is good. All you have to do is entertain them for a couple of hours each day by reading to them and doing the odd magic trick. I know how good you are with kids so I thought you'd jump at it. There's an audition tomorrow at four pm at the church hall in Boronia Avenue, not far from here.'

'OK, I'll be there, but I would still like to know why you—'

'Great, I'll put in a good word for you. I'll text you all the details. Good luck.'

'Roberta—' Mia began but the agent interrupted her again, making up some excuse that she had an important call coming in.

'Sorry, Mia. Gotta go. Let me know how you get on. Bye.'

Mia stared at the phone in her hand, her brow furrowing slightly.

It rang a few minutes later and she was not at all surprised to hear Bryn's voice informing her that Henry would be collecting her for their dinner engagement that evening.

'Sorry about that, Mia,' he said. 'But I've got some legal work to see to over my great-aunt's estate. It will save time if Henry brings you straight to the restaurant. I've booked it for seven-thirty and I should be there soon after if all goes well.'

'Why don't we eat here instead?' she suggested, wondering if what she had to say would be fit for the ears of other diners.

'No, I gave Marita a couple of days off, as one of her kids is sick. Don't worry, I'll be there as soon as I can. How was your day by the way?'

'Wonderful,' she lied. 'I had my hair done and went shopping; I even bought a dress for tonight.'

'You sound like you're looking forward to seeing me,' he said at her light and cheery tone.

'Of course I am,' she said. 'I have so much to tell you. I can hardly wait.'

There was a tiny pause before he asked, 'What have you got to tell me?'

'It's a surprise,' she said. 'I'll see you tonight.'

'Mia…'

The sound of the doorbell gave her a perfect excuse to end the call. 'Oops, got to go. It sounds like there's someone at the door.'

'It's a present for you,' he said. 'I hope you like it.'

'How sweet,' she said, grinding her teeth. 'I'll see you later. Bye.'

She opened the door to find a florist delivery-service man with a huge bunch of tall red roses and a slim box wrapped in pink tissue with a white bow around it. 'Mrs Mia Dwyer?'

'Yes, that's me,' she said, mentally tacking on: *but not for much longer.*

'These are for you.' He handed them over and smiled. 'Hey, I've never met a really famous person before. Can I have your autograph?'

She blinked at him. '*My* autograph?'

'Yeah, my two kids loved you in that ad you did with the puppy and the toilet rolls. They'll be tickled pink to hear I've met you in person.'

She put the roses down and rummaged for something to sign her name on and, asking for his children's names, scribbled a greeting and drew a big smiley face beside each one. 'Here you are.' She handed it to him with a smile.

'My wife listens to your husband's programme,' he said. 'She reckons it's the most romantic thing how you two got together.'

'Yes...yes, it was.'

'Well, I'd better be going. Nice meeting you.'

'And you,' she said.

She waited until he'd driven away before

picking up the roses and the box and carried them inside. She unpinned the card and, taking it from the tiny envelope, opened it to read the message. It said: 'I hope you like these. See you tonight, Bryn.'

She frowned as she put it to one side and opened the tissue-wrapped box, where inside was an exquisite string of pearls resting on a bed of plush blue velvet.

Anger bubbled up inside her. No doubt this was his parting gift, a stupid bunch of roses and expensive pearls to soften the blow of him calling an end to their marriage.

She went to the kitchen and, taking a pair of scissors out of the utensil drawer, came back to where she'd left the roses and one by one snipped off each perfect, fragrant bud, leaving the tall stalks standing looking forlorn and headless.

She then picked up the string of pearls and snipped her way along it until they rolled like marbles all over the tiled foyer. She gave a satisfied little sigh as the last one rolled underneath the hall stand.

It would probably take him months to retrieve them all.

* * *

Mia ferried her bags over to Gina's and, leaving her car there on the final trip, caught a taxi back to Bryn's house to dress for the evening. She was ready and waiting when Henry arrived, and, quickly closing the door behind her, followed him out to the car.

'You look very beautiful this evening, Mrs Dywer,' he said as he helped her settle inside the car. 'Mr Dwyer is going to be knocked sideways when he sees you, I'm sure.'

She gave him a sugar-sweet smile. 'That's the plan. I can't have him thinking he married a woman with no taste or style, now, can I?'

'You are the perfect wife for him, if you don't mind me saying,' he said once they were on their way. 'Mr Dwyer has had a hard time of it but since you came into his life I've noticed some real changes. He would never have coped so well with his great-aunt's death without your help. You're good for him.'

'Thank you, Henry,' she said softly, desperately trying to control the urge to cry.

The restaurant was on the harbour in Rushcutters Bay and although it was crowded the table Bryn had booked for them was tucked away in a quiet corner.

She was sitting at the table with a glass of champagne in front of her, mentally rehearsing her performance, when Bryn arrived. She watched him exchange a few words with the *maître d'* before looking in her direction, his dark blue eyes meshing with hers.

She watched as every head turned as he wove his way through the restaurant to where she was sitting, bending his head to place a soft kiss to her forehead before he took the seat opposite. She held her breath as his gaze dipped to her unadorned neck.

'Did you get my gift?' he asked.

'Yes, thank you. They were…beautiful.'

'You're not wearing the pearls.'

'I had trouble with the clasp,' she said. 'I thought I might lose them if I didn't do it up properly.'

He seemed satisfied with her answer and smiled as the waiter approached with the menu and wine list.

'How did your meeting go?' she asked once the waiter had taken Bryn's request for a bottle of cabernet sauvignon.

'It was fine,' he answered. 'I had some papers to sign, that's all.'

'How about your meeting with your producer this morning? Was that productive?'

He waited until the waiter had poured their wine before answering. 'Yes...it was.'

Mia watched as he toyed with his glass, staring into its blood-red contents as if wondering how they came to be there.

'I had a phone call from my ex-agent today,' she said into the silence.

'Oh?' He took a sip of wine.

'Yes; apparently she's found some work for me. Isn't that nice?'

His eyes fell away from hers as he leaned back in his chair for the waiter to place some hot bread rolls on the table.

'And here I was, thinking she thought I was hopeless,' she went on once the waiter had gone. 'I lost so much confidence when she and Theodore dropped me but it seems she thinks I have some measure of talent after all.'

'There's never been any question of your having talent,' Bryn said, meeting her eyes. 'I should never have written the review in the first place. God knows I've regretted it ever since.'

'No, you shouldn't,' she said. 'But then there are a lot of things you shouldn't have done, aren't there, Bryn?'

He held her gaze for a tense moment, his throat moving up and down slightly.

'Mia, the reason we are here now is because I have a confession to make. I should have told you in the first place but I had no idea I would end up feeling this way. I didn't see it coming. I should have but I didn't. I guess I didn't want to.'

Mia waited for him to continue, her fingers tightening around her untouched glass of red wine, her anger building so steadily she hardly took in what he was saying. She just wanted to say her piece and get away before he had the chance to hurt her further.

'I don't think it's fair to continue our relationship on the terms I laid down,' he said. 'I think it's time I told you the truth about how I engineered our marriage.'

It was just the cue she'd been waiting for. 'You mean about how you insisted Theo drop me from the play?'

He frowned. 'So you know about that?'

'Yes, and I also know how you told Roberta to stop finding me work so you could force me to act your little role for you,' she continued. 'It had nothing to do with your ratings, did it, Bryn? It had more to do with you wanting to secure a fortune for yourself. It was clever, I admit, and if I were the gullible, innocent fool you seem to think I am I would have fallen for it.'

He stared at her speechlessly as she went on, 'You see, Bryn, I knew what you were up to. I decided to teach *you* a lesson. You thought I couldn't act to save myself but in the end I completely fooled you and everyone else as well with my convincing performance.'

His eyes narrowed slightly. 'What do you mean?'

She gave him a cat-that-swallowed-the-canary smile. 'I'm not really in love with you, Bryn. And I wasn't a virgin either. How was that for a performance? Brilliant, don't you think? You fell for it hook, line and sinker. God, how I was laughing at you the whole time! You thought I couldn't act but boy, did I show you.'

His features became rigid and white-tipped with anger, his eyes like dark blue diamonds as they clashed with hers. 'You bitch. You lying little bitch. And here I was, feeling guilty for using you.'

She gave him a cold look of disdain. 'You didn't use me, Bryn. I used you. I got the leg-up to fame I needed. People are stopping me for my autograph now. How cool is that? And all because of you. I guess I should be thanking you for giving my career the boost it needed, but do you know what, I think I'll make a toast to you instead?' She got to her feet and raised her glass of red wine. 'Here's to the end of our temporary marriage.' She gave him an imperious smile. 'Cheers, Bryn. Thanks for the memories—I'm going to be dining out on those for years,' she said and tipped the contents of her glass into his lap.

As exits went it was one of her best. She wove her way through the tables with a smile of victory plastered to her face, raising her hand to him in a tiny fingertip wave as a taxi pulled into the kerb outside the restaurant.

Her last sight of him was the absolute look of incredulity on his face as he got to his feet, the red wine over his groin looking as if someone had stabbed him.

The taxi driver looked at her in the rear-view mirror. 'Hey, don't I know you? I think I saw you in the paper the other day. You're famous, right?'

Mia gave him a tight little smile. 'Yes, I am. But guess what? It's not all it's cracked up to be.' And she promptly burst into tears.

CHAPTER SIXTEEN

'Wow, an audition at last!' Gina crowed with delight the following afternoon. 'This is just what you need to take your mind off you-know-who. What's this one for?'

Mia put the final touches to her pixie costume, marvelling yet again at the pointy silicone ears which looked so real. 'Roberta organised it for me.'

'But I thought she wasn't representing you any more.'

'Yes, well, maybe she had a twinge of conscience, because she rang and told me she had an audition lined up for me. She told me I was perfect for the role.'

Gina peered at Mia's ears. *'A pixie?'*

'Not just any old pixie,' Mia said. 'If I get the job I'm going to be officially known at the Pain Pixie.'

'The Pain Pixie?' Gina wrinkled her nose. 'That sounds a bit weird.'

'No, it's a fabulous idea,' Mia said. 'The Pain Pixie visits sick kids in hospital, reading to them and entertaining them to take their minds off their pain. I've even got a pot of pixie dust, see?' She sprinkled some in the air. 'And a wand.' She waved it about for a moment, privately wishing it could bring about the miracle she wanted in her own life.

'You're right, that does sound fabulous,' Gina said. 'What time is your audition?'

She glanced at her watch. 'I'm going now. Wish me luck.'

Mia knocked on the door of the church hall half an hour later and was greeted by a woman who asked her to stand on the stage and read from a well-known children's book.

She did as she was told, reading in a clear, animated voice.

'Thank you, that's great,' the woman said before Mia had even finished the page. 'You're perfect for the role. You can start this afternoon. I'll give you the schedule with all the contact times. You will be paid a wage plus travel expenses.'

Mia stepped down from the stage and took the sheet the woman handed her. 'Is that all you want me to do?' she asked. 'I mean, I can do accents and tell jokes and that sort of stuff.'

'No, you're fine. You've got the job. You came with very high recommendations.'

As auditions went it was certainly the easiest Mia had ever experienced, she thought as she made her way back to Gina's.

'How did it go?' Gina asked.

'I got the job,' she said with a little frown.

'What's wrong? You don't seem all that thrilled. Isn't it what you were expecting?'

'I don't know...' she said. 'I'm just getting a funny feeling about this.'

'What do you mean? Don't you like the sound of the work?'

'No,' she said. 'It's a dream job. I get paid to make kids happy. I can't think of anything I'd like better, but still...'

'You're still thinking about him, aren't you?' Gina said softly.

'I'm trying not to...'

'I heard him on the radio,' Gina said.

Mia felt herself tensing. 'Was he his usual cutting self?'

'Actually, no, he wasn't.'

'What did he say?'

'Nothing much, he just played a whole lot of soppy romantic songs instead of that usual stuff he plays.'

Mia gave a little snort. 'He's just trying to make his listeners feel sorry for him. No doubt it will lift his ratings to an all-time high.'

'You could well be right because his ratings have toppled Maxwell Murdoch's from the rival channel for the first time in years,' Gina said. 'But it's funny in a way because I read in the paper that Bryn is not renewing his contract at the station.'

Mia's lip curled cynically. 'That's because he's so filthy rich now he's got his hands on his great-aunt's estate.'

'Not according to his column in this morning's paper,' Gina said. 'He said he'd given the whole proceeds of his great-aunt's estate to a well-known children's charity. It was finalised with his lawyers yesterday.'

Mia stared at her flatmate for several heart-stopping seconds. 'Do you still have the paper?'

'It's here somewhere...' Gina began to search for it, finally unearthing it from beneath the sofa cushions. 'Here.' She pressed it out flat for Mia to read.

Mia read the column, her heart beginning to thud unevenly in her chest.

'What's wrong?' Gina asked. 'You look like you're about to faint.'

'No...no, I'm fine...' She forced a smile to her stiff lips. 'I'm just nervous about my first session at the hospital.'

Mia turned up at the hospital as arranged and was led to the children's ward, where she spent an enjoyable hour or two reading and playing with the young patients. She couldn't believe how rewarding it was to see each child's face light up when she came in. It was the most rewarding role she had ever played and she didn't want it to ever end.

If only someone could sprinkle some pixie dust over her and take her own pain away, she thought as she made her way to the next child's bedside.

'Are you really a pixie?' a little boy with wide, dark brown eyes asked.

'Of course I am,' Mia insisted. 'See my pot of magic dust? This is what I sprinkle around to take pain away. It has special magic powers.'

He gave her a sceptical look. 'Does it really work?'

'How's your pain been while I've been here?' she asked.

He smiled at her, showing his missing front teeth. 'I haven't even thought about it.'

'See?' She gave him a grin. 'That's what I'm here for.'

She went next to a little girl who'd had extensive chemotherapy for acute myeloid leukaemia. The sight of the frail seven-year-old with no hair struck at Mia's heart and she sat down by the bed and started talking to her. She found out the little girl's name was Ellie, the very same as her sister's.

'It's short for Eleanor,' the little girl informed her. 'But I still have trouble spelling it so I much prefer Ellie.'

'I can't say I blame you,' Mia said. 'I have an adopted sister whose name is Eleanora. That's even harder to spell. We've always called her Ellie.'

'I don't have any sisters,' the little Ellie said. 'I have a brother but he's only two.'

'This must be tough for you in here,' Mia said. 'I've heard your parents live in the country on a farm. It must be hard not having regular visitors.'

'It's nice that you're here,' the little girl said. 'Is it true you have magic powers?'

Mia felt like the biggest fraud in history but something about the little girl's dark blue eyes reminded her of Bryn and she found herself confessing, 'I have the ability to take pain away with the wave of my magic wand. That's why I'm called the Pain Pixie.' She pulled out her wand and waved it in the air. 'But I have to let you in on a little secret. It only works if the patient really wants to get rid of the pain.'

'I'm not in pain right now but I feel sad that my parents can't always be here with me,' Ellie said. 'Do you think your magic wand can help with that?'

Mia felt as if her heart was being clamped by an industrial-strength vice. 'I can be here as often as you need me to be here,' she said, fighting back tears. 'I can read to you, watch DVDs with you or sit and talk to you as long as you want.'

'Really?' The little girl's eyes lit up like bright little diamonds.

Mia smiled and, reaching out, squeezed the little girl's hand ever so gently. 'That's what the Pain Pixie's job is all about. I'll be here for you whenever you need me and if I'm off with another patient you have only to tell the nurse on duty so I can get back here as soon as possible.'

'I feel better already,' little Ellie said. 'I'm so happy you've come to visit me. I don't miss my mummy so much now.'

Mia bent forward and pressed a soft kiss to the little girl's forehead. 'You know something, Ellie? I'm a whole lot older than you but I still sometimes miss my mum. You're a very brave girl.'

'I'm not really very brave,' Ellie confessed. 'I cried heaps last night.'

It was on the tip of Mia's tongue to confess the same but somehow she stopped herself in time.

A few minutes later a nurse came over to her to inform her of a patient in a private room who particularly needed her attention.

'I'm afraid this is a very tragic case,' the nurse said in grave tones. 'I'm not sure you'll be able to do much to help the poor darling boy but it's worth a try.'

'What happened to him?' Mia asked in an undertone.

'Heart trouble,' the nurse answered, shaking her head sadly.

'Is it a congenital condition?' Mia asked, thinking of the heart murmur her father had had since birth.

'He's had it since he was a little boy, I believe,' the nurse said and indicated the door of the private room. 'But evidently the problem has become more serious of late. Go on in, he's expecting you.'

Mia gave the door a little knock and opened it to find Bryn sitting on the edge of the single bed. She stared at him for several moments, her mouth opening and closing in shock.

She took a step backwards but he sprang off the bed and captured her before she could get away, closing the door so no one could listen in. 'No, don't go, Mia. I want to talk to you.'

'Let me go, you...you...' She was so furious she couldn't think of a bad enough word to flay him with. 'I should have known you'd be behind this! How *could* you? I really love this job and now I find, like everything else to do with you, it's all a stupid act!'

'I had to see you,' he said. 'I need to tell you how much I love you. And this job is genuine. It's yours as long as you want it.'

She stared at him with wide eyes, her heart beginning to hammer unevenly. 'You're ...you're sure?'

'Yes, Mia, I'm sure. The job's yours.'

She moistened her mouth, her eyes still focused on his. 'I—I mean about the...the I-love-you bit...'

He smiled as he drew her closer. 'I fell in love with you the very first day I met you but I was too stupid to see it. I guess I didn't want to admit it. I hated feeling so vulnerable. But believe me, Mia. I love you. I can't imagine life without you. When I went home after our dinner I was so angry at what you'd said it took me a while to realise the clues you'd left behind that made me realise how you really felt.'

'You mean the roses and the pearls?'

His eyes glinted with amusement. 'Agnes is probably turning over in her grave at what you did to her precious pearls.'

'Oh, my God!' She put her hand up to her throat. 'They belonged to your great-aunt?'

'She left them for you in her will. They're worth a small fortune, or at least they will be when I finally find them all and have them restrung.'

She gave him a shamefaced look. 'I was so angry. I thought you were giving them to me as a consolation prize to mark the end of our temporary marriage.'

'Can you ever forgive me for what I did?' he asked. 'I was wrong to have you dropped from the company, and as for getting Roberta to stop representing you…well, all I can say is I'm deeply ashamed of myself. I didn't stop to think of how you would be affected. I just wanted you so badly I was prepared to put aside every other consideration so I could have you. As for my great-aunt's estate, I never wanted it for myself but I just couldn't bear the thought of giving it to the man who had killed my parents. My great-aunt was right, though; it is time I learnt to let go of the past and forgive the poor man. He didn't do it intentionally and has paid for that one error of judgement all of his life.'

'It's all right,' she said. 'I don't think I was right for that play either. To tell you the truth I haven't been all that happy with any of the roles

I've had in the past. All of my life I've been searching for something to do that really makes a difference and today I found it.' She looked up at him with hope shining in her eyes. 'Do you really mean this job is for real?'

'Of course it is,' he said. 'I'd been thinking about it for ages. I once spent a week in hospital not long after my parents died. I had my tonsils out. I was so lonely and afraid, I have never forgotten it. I swore one day I would try and do something to help kids who were sick.'

She smiled up at him. 'So you became a principle sponsor for a major children's charity even though you pretend you're not capable of love.'

'You have taught me how to love, Mia,' he said, 'and not only that, you taught me how to recognise it. If you hadn't come along and tossed that coffee in my lap I might have very well ended up alone and lonely for the rest of my life. No one has ever affected me the way you do. I looked into those big grey eyes of yours and I was totally lost. It was a frightening experience for someone like me who has clung to what is predictable and controllable all his life. When you told me you loved me I was so overcome, I felt so guilty for what I had done. I couldn't imagine you ever forgiving me.'

'Of course I forgive you—I love you. I think I fell in love with you the first day too. But I had my own reasons for marrying you which had nothing to do with how I felt about you.'

'You did?'

She gave him a sheepish look. 'I would never have agreed to take things so far but Ellie was in trouble in South America. She needed money in a hurry and your marriage proposal was the ideal way to solve a problem I just couldn't solve on my own. It was only as we were officially married that I started to realise that I had got myself in a little deeper than I'd initially intended.'

'So will you agree to stay married to me for real? No acting this time?'

She gave him an impish smile, two tiny dimples appearing in her cheeks. 'I wasn't acting in the first place.'

'You know something, sweetheart?' he said as he brought his mouth down to hers. 'Nor was I.'

MILLS & BOON® PUBLISH EIGHT LARGE PRINT TITLES A MONTH. THESE ARE THE EIGHT TITLES FOR APRIL 2007

———— ❦ ————

THE CHRISTMAS BRIDE
Penny Jordan

RELUCTANT MISTRESS, BLACKMAILED WIFE
Lynne Graham

AT THE GREEK TYCOON'S PLEASURE
Cathy Williams

THE VIRGIN'S PRICE
Melanie Milburne

THE BRIDE OF MONTEFALCO
Rebecca Winters

CRAZY ABOUT THE BOSS
Teresa Southwick

CLAIMING THE CATTLEMAN'S HEART
Barbara Hannay

BLIND-DATE MARRIAGE
Fiona Harper

MILLS & BOON®

Live the emotion

0307 Rom LP

MILLS & BOON® PUBLISH EIGHT LARGE PRINT TITLES A MONTH. THESE ARE THE EIGHT TITLES FOR MAY 2007

THE ITALIAN'S FUTURE BRIDE
Michelle Reid

PLEASURED IN THE BILLIONAIRE'S BED
Miranda Lee

BLACKMAILED BY DIAMONDS, BOUND BY MARRIAGE
Sarah Morgan

THE GREEK BOSS'S BRIDE
Chantelle Shaw

OUTBACK MAN SEEKS WIFE
Margaret Way

THE NANNY AND THE SHEIKH
Barbara McMahon

THE BUSINESSMAN'S BRIDE
Jackie Braun

MEANT-TO-BE MOTHER
Ally Blake

MILLS & BOON®

0407 Rom